USBORNE

Sandy Lane Stables

Runaway Pony

Susannah Leigh

USBORNE

First published in 1996 by Usborne Publishing Ltd, Usborne House,
83-85 Saffron Hill, London EC1N 8RT, England.
www.usborne.com

First published in America 1997. AE

ISBN 0 7945 0507 4 (paperback)

Typeset in Times

Printed in Great Britain

Editor: Michelle Bates
Series Editor: Gaby Waters
Designer: Lucy Smith
Cover Design: Neil Francis
Map Illustrations by: John Woodcock
Cover Photograph supplied by: Horsepix

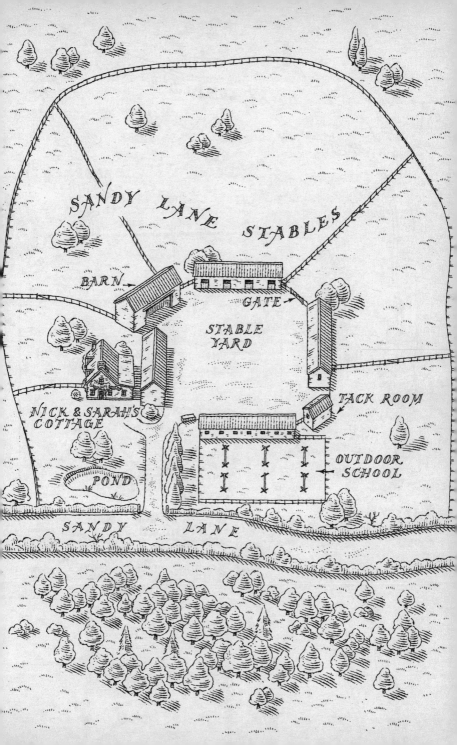

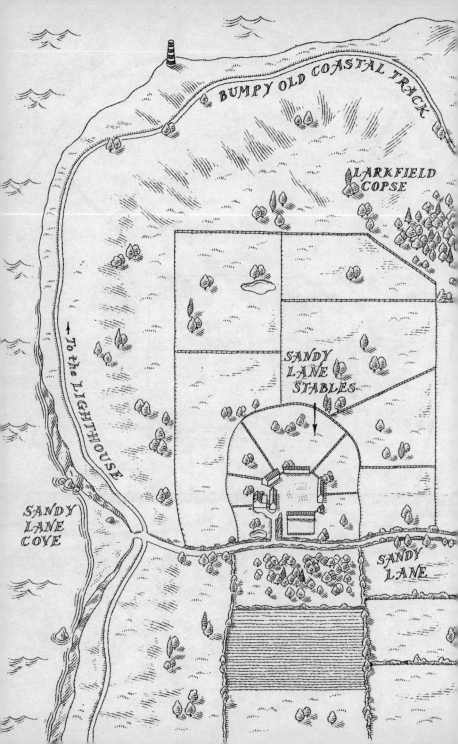

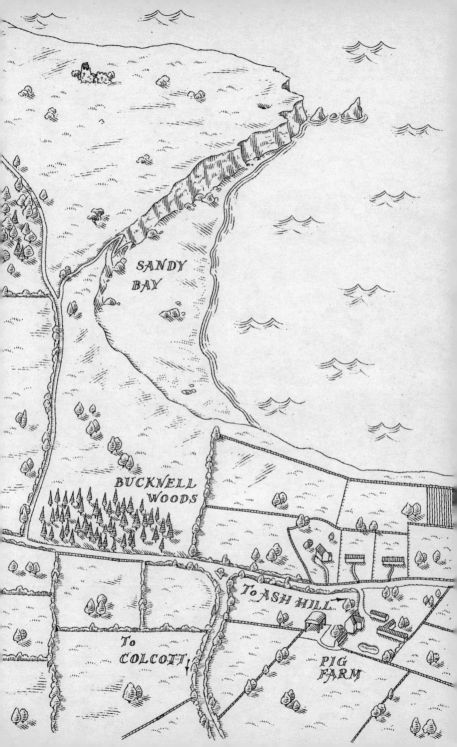

SANDY
BAY

BUCKNELL
WOODS

To ASH HILL

To
COLCOTT

PIG
FARM

CONTENTS

1

THE RUNAWAY PONY

Jess Adams free-wheeled her bicycle down the gentle hill. "No more school!" she cheered as she sped past the fields. "Hooray for the Spring break!"

She turned sharply into the drive of Sandy Lane Stables and skidded the bike to a halt. It was early morning, not quite seven o'clock, and no one else was around. Only the ponies were awake, shuffling in their stalls and whinnying softly for their breakfasts. Jess cast a glance at the little stone house tucked away behind the stables.

"I bet Nick and Sarah won't be up for hours," she said to herself.

Nick and Sarah Brooks were the owners of Sandy Lane. Last night had been a rare evening off. They had gone to a charity dinner dance.

"It's in aid of the *SPCA*," Sarah had said as she twirled excitedly around the stables, the emerald satin of her borrowed evening gown matching her green eyes.

"You'll probably be dancing till midnight," Jess had sighed. "Sipping pink champagne and slurping caviar."

"Probably," Nick had said as he adjusted his black bow tie.

"And you're bound to be back very late and be really tired in the morning," Jess had continued, forking the last of the hay into Minstrel's hayfeeder. "So perhaps I ought to come in early and start the ponies' breakfasts for you. And then maybe..."

"...Maybe you could have a free ride later on in the day?" Nick smiled and finished the sentence for her. Money was tight in Jess's family since her dad had lost his job. There wasn't much spare cash for her riding lessons.

"You can have the eleven o'clock ride for free," Nick had said in an understanding voice. "I'll *even* try to be up and around early tomorrow morning to give you a hand..."

That was last night. And now it was morning and Nick wasn't up. But Jess had learned a lot in the two years she had been coming to Sandy Lane. She certainly knew enough to start getting the ponies ready for the day.

"Perhaps Nick will even let me ride *you* this afternoon, you beautiful pony," she said as she drew nearer to Storm Cloud's stall.

Storm Cloud, a dappled-gray Arab, greeted Jess eagerly, poking her delicate, dished face over the stall door. Jess slipped her the sugar cube she had been saving especially for her. She had never seen a pony so breathtaking.

She thought back to the day Nick had first found Storm Cloud at the Ash Hill Horse Sale. Storm Cloud had been weak and neglected, but even then Nick had been able to see the pony's potential. And with love and patience, he had brought her back to her former glory. She was a natural jumper and it wouldn't be long before she was competing.

In Jess's mind, Storm Cloud was the best pony at the stables. She might look fragile, but she was really gutsy and strong-willed. Whenever Jess had been lucky enough to ride her, she had felt as though they had the potential to do anything; jump any fence, outrun any other pony. She loved to imagine jumping Storm Cloud in a show and riding off with the championship trophy, although she had never told anyone else this dream. It was her secret.

"What a team we'd make, eh Stormy?" Jess whispered into the pony's ear. Storm Cloud neighed gently in reply and at the same time, Jess heard a whinny from a nearby stall. She grinned as Minstrel, the little skewbald pony, showed his big yellow teeth and rolled the whites of his eyes at her.

"Don't worry Minstrel," Jess laughed. "I haven't forgotten about you."

Minstrel was Jess's regular pony at Sandy Lane –

3

the one she rode the most. He was a good, solid riding school pony and Jess was very fond of him.

"I guess I'll be riding you later on, Minstrel," Jess began as she made her way over to the pony's stall. "Bet you can't wait..."

"Come here!"

Angry shouting and the crunch of hooves on gravel stopped Jess in her tracks and made her spin around sharply. Careening toward her down the drive, wild-eyed with fear and long tail flying behind, was a palomino pony. It was completely out of control. Jess's heart began to pound and her breath came in sharp gasps, but almost without thinking she held out her arms.

"Whoa, little pony," she said, as calmly as she could. "Slow down."

Jess stood her ground and now the pony was only inches away from her. At the sound of Jess's voice it clattered to a halt. It dropped its head and nuzzled a velvety nose into Jess's shoulder. Jess sighed with relief. The next moment she had located a stray mint in the depths of her pocket. Gingerly she fished it out and offered it to the palomino. The pony, a pretty little mare of about 14 hands, crunched contentedly. For a brief moment, girl and pony stood nose to nose talking softly to one another, the white-gold of the pony's mane contrasting sharply with Jess's own dark curls.

"Come back you!" A stocky man ran up behind the pony. His face was red from shouting and he was panting hard. In his hand he waved a muddy halter.

The pony started, but Jess calmed it with a steadying hand.

When the man saw Jess he gasped. "Thanks! Thanks a lot. You've saved my hide."

"That's all right," Jess said, trying to sound as if catching runaway ponies was something she did every day.

"Well you were very brave," the man acknowledged. "It couldn't have been easy standing your ground like that."

Jess shrugged her shoulders in what she hoped was a casual way. She couldn't help stealing a glance at the house in case Nick or Sarah happened to be looking out. She was sure they would have been impressed by her actions. But there was still no sign of them.

The pony butted her nose against Jess's shoulder. Jess laughed.

"She's lovely," she cried, gently pulling the pony's ears. "What's her name?"

"Um... Goldie." The man leaned forward and put his hands on his knees. He took deep breaths. "Because her coat shimmers like gold," he finished.

"She looks as precious as gold, too. Don't you, pretty girl?" Jess turned to the pony again.

"She may look like an angel," the man agreed grumpily. "But she's a devil to catch. I was trying to load her into the trailer when she bolted. I'm parked miles back up the road..."

"She probably caught the scent of the horses here and decided to investigate," said Jess.

"You could be right," the man replied. "It's a good thing you were here to stop her. She's not my pony... she belongs to my daughter. I'm no good with the animal–" the man stopped abruptly. "Anyway, I can't stand around here talking all day. I've got to get this pony back." He moved swiftly toward the palomino who started and shied away.

"She won't let me catch her," he muttered.

"Here, let me try," said Jess, holding out her hand for the halter. Talking gently to the pony and murmuring words of encouragement, she stroked the mare's nose firmly with her left hand while deftly slipping on the halter with her right. Goldie didn't flinch. Taking the lead rope in her hand, Jess turned back to the man as he let out a low whistle.

"Good job. You've been a real help. A real help," he repeated softly. He tugged at the lead rope and this time the pony trotted obediently behind.

Jess stood watching as they disappeared out of sight. Now that they had gone she felt strangely deflated. She thought of all the other questions she had wanted to ask the man. Where was Goldie kept? Why didn't his daughter catch the pony herself?

Minstrel whinnied loudly from his stall, cutting into her thoughts.

"All right boy." Jess dragged her mind away from the palomino. "It's breakfast time. Now, what shall it be this morning? Hay or bacon and eggs?"

2

NICK HAS SOME NEWS

"Finish your cereal for goodness sake, Jess." Her mother looked on in exasperation as Jess pushed the soggy cornflakes around the bowl.

"Sorry Mom, I was miles away." Jess lifted her head from her hand and yawned loudly. Going to the stables so early and having to come home for breakfast had been more tiring than she'd imagined.

"What time did you leave the house this morning?" her mother asked, shaking her head.

"Six... six thirty," Jess answered nonchalantly.

"And on the first day of break, too." Her brother, Jack, looked up from his toast with a mixture of disgust and disbelief. "You're crazy, Jess."

Jess's mother sighed loudly and continued her lecture. "You spend far too much time at those stables,

Jess. I hope you don't think you're going to be down there every day of your break. What about your homework?"

Jess sank down in her chair. She knew it was no use trying to explain how completely and totally necessary ponies were to her life. Instead she gobbled down the rest of her cereal and bolted for the door.

"I've got a ride at eleven. It's free," she explained hastily, "in return for the work I did this morning."

Her mother accepted defeat. "Oh Jess... if only you spent as much time on your schoolwork as you did at those stables," she sighed. "Don't be back late."

"I won't," Jess promised. "See you later. Bye!"

Jess grabbed her bicycle from the tiny front yard and tried to put her mother's remarks out of her mind. She didn't want to think about school work – not now... not when the sun was shining and there were ponies to ride. As she rode away from her house in Colcott, she thought again about Goldie, the palomino pony that had run into Sandy Lane that morning. Soon she had drifted off into a daydream. In her mind she wasn't pedaling along the road to Sandy Lane, but cantering cross-country. As she swung into the stables' driveway the rusty red bicycle beneath her was a beautiful pony. Just the lightest touch on the reins was all that was needed...

"Look out!"

Jess snapped awake from her dream just in time to see her friend, Tom, pushing a wheelbarrow full of hay directly across her path. She slammed on the brakes and her trusty steed, now a rusty red bicycle once again, swerved to the left and screeched to a halt.

"Whew. That was a close one," Jess gasped, just managing to stay upright on her bike. She blushed, flustered. "Sorry Tom, I was daydreaming."

"That's OK," Tom grinned and pushed away the strand of brown hair that had fallen across his face. He walked off, whistling softly to himself.

Jess shook her head. Of all the people to look clumsy in front of, why did it have to be Tom? He was definitely the best rider at Sandy Lane. He even had his own horse, Chancey, who was kept on half-board at Sandy Lane. Although Chancey was ridden by everyone, he really only had eyes for Tom. Jess sighed, turning her bicycle toward the tack room.

"Hey Jess, hang on a moment!" Her best friend, Rosie, came pedaling up the drive, her blond ponytail flying in the breeze. "Have you been here all morning?"

"No, I went home for breakfast," Jess smiled.

"Did you earn yourself a free ride?" Rosie asked.

"Yes. I'm going on the eleven o'clock trail ride. And something else happened too," Jess said to Rosie. "I made friends with a new pony."

"A new pony?" Rosie was immediately interested. "Where? Whose?"

"It was a palomino mare," Jess began. "Her name's Goldie. She came running into the stables."

"A palomino," Rosie sighed. "How lovely."

"I had to hold out my arms and stop her, Rosie,"

Jess said proudly. "She was charging toward me, really, really fast."

"You're lucky she didn't trample you," Rosie shivered. "Why was she running into Sandy Lane anyway?"

Jess explained about the man chasing the palomino. "The pony belongs to his daughter. He didn't seem to know much about it at all..."

Now they had reached the fence beside the tack room. All the regular junior Sandy Lane riders chained their bicycles here. There was Tom's green racer, and Charlie's new and shiny black mountain bike too. Rosie parked her bike neatly and Jess dumped hers down on the ground next to it.

"Come on you two, be careful when you park your bikes." Nick Brooks appeared on the steps of the tack room, blinking painfully in the bright April sunshine. "This is a stable, not a junk yard."

"Oops, my fault," said Jess, swiftly straightening her bike.

"Sorry I wasn't up to help you out this morning, Jess," Nick smiled ruefully. "I think I'm getting too old for this dancing-all-night nonsense. My legs are killing me," he groaned. "Anyway I've managed to put the list for the eleven o'clock ride up on the bulletin board. You're on Minstrel." Nick wandered off, limping slightly.

"I hope I'm on Pepper," Rosie said as she followed Jess into the tack room. "Cool," she continued as she ran her hand down the list of riders and ponies and saw her name next to Pepper's.

"I don't know what you see in that pony," Jess wrinkled up her nose. "He's so stubborn."

"Only with everyone else," Rosie reasoned. "He's always been a dream with me."

"It's because you're such a fantastic rider," Charlie teased as he entered the tack room, running a hand through his grubby blond hair. Rosie gave an embarrassed laugh, but Jess was quiet. Charlie was right about Rosie. She was a fantastic rider, even if she was too modest to admit it.

Jess didn't begrudge Rosie her riding ability. She was pleased for her best friend, but she couldn't help feeling envious of Rosie's skill, which lay in her calmness and poise. When Rosie sat on a horse she looked completely in control.

Not like me, Jess thought now. Hands flapping everywhere, feet slipping out of the stirrups.

"You're a good rider, Jess," Nick had often commented, "But it's your style that lets you down. Try and be slightly less messy when you ride."

Rosie was never messy, thought Jess. She was neat, and patient too. Maybe that's why Pepper responded so well to her.

But *I* had patience this morning, Jess thought to herself. And I was calm, too. I couldn't have stopped that runaway pony if I hadn't been...

"Hey!" Jess's thoughts were interrupted as Rosie tapped her lightly with a crop.

"You're supposed to use that on the ponies, not me!"

11

Jess said indignantly.

"You need a little of waking up today, Jess," Rosie laughed. "I must have asked you five times to pass the hoof pick. Didn't you hear me? Come on, it's almost eleven. We'll be late for our ride."

"Sorry. I was dreaming about that beautiful palomino."

"I wonder why we've never seen her around here before," Rosie said as they left the tack room. "Is she stabled nearby?"

"I'm not sure," Jess admitted as they reached Minstrel's stall. She paused at the door and absent-mindedly patted the pony's neck. He bent his head and pushed his nose into her shoulder.

Rosie moved away toward Pepper's stall. "I'd better get a move on," she called. "See you when I've tacked up. What did you do with that hoofpick by the way?"

"What? Oh, it's still in my hand, sorry." Jess handed the pick to Rosie and unbolted Minstrel's door. She tacked him up quickly and went to join the rest of the riders in front of the stables. Tom was there on the back of Chancey and Charlie waved down at Jess from Napoleon, a huge horse of 16.2 hands.

"My dad took me out to dinner at that new restaurant near Ash Hill last night," Charlie called as he leaned forward in the saddle. "You know, the one where they play all those music videos in the background. It was amazing."

Jess flashed Charlie a smile. He was always trying to show off, but she didn't mind. She knew things hadn't been too easy for him since the divorce. He didn't see much of his dad these days.

"Sounds great," she said. "Lucky you."

"Come on you guys," a voice interrupted their conversation.

It was Sarah. She was taking the trail ride out and waited patiently by the gate. There were dark shadows under her eyes, but she was smiling happily. "Let's get going."

In no time at all, the riders were out of the stable grounds and walking in single file down the lane. Sarah rode Storm Cloud as she led them up the bumpy old coastal track toward the lighthouse. Jess could already feel Minstrel chomping at the bit.

"OK, let's gallop across the grass. It's nice and flat," Sarah called out as they neared the lighthouse. "We'll head toward Larkfield Copse. Stop on the edge of it and don't let the ponies run away with you. We don't want anyone scalped by the trees. Right then, at my signal."

Then they were off, galloping across the field. Jess gave Minstrel his head and they flew across the ground. Thundering to a stop where the grass met the trees, Jess gave a whoop of joy. There was nothing to match the feeling of being out on a pony on a crisp, clear day.

"Pepper's going great," Rosie cried as she drew alongside Jess.

"So's Minstrel," Jess replied. "Isn't this fantastic?"

At the end of the hour, the ride wound its way back

to the stables. As they back into the stable grounds and dismounted, Alex and Kate Hardy, the last of the regular junior riders, came running up to greet them.

"Where have you two been?" Jess called out as she put up Minstrel's stirrups. "Weren't you booked on the eleven o'clock ride?"

"No, I've got a lunchtime lesson," Kate replied, giving Minstrel a pat. "And Alex is riding later."

"Well you missed an awesome ride," Rosie joined in as she led Pepper away.

"But it was a good thing I was here," Kate replied mysteriously. "We've got pony trouble afoot!"

Jess laughed. Kate could be a little dramatic sometimes. "What *are* you talking about, Kate? It sounds exciting."

"Not really," Kate admitted. "It's a kind of a sad story really. A girl came into the yard, about ten minutes ago. Her pony's missing and she wondered if anyone had seen it. Apparently she keeps it in a field a few miles up the road and this morning when this girl, Belinda..."

"Just spit it out, Kate." Alex barged in on his sister's conversation. "What happened is – this girl, Belinda, went to get her pony from its field this morning and it wasn't there. Vanished. The gate was open so it must have escaped."

"What's it look like?" Charlie joined in the conversation.

"What's it called?" Tom asked:

"Um, it's a palomino mare apparently," Alex said.

"Goes by the name of Golddust."

Jess was immediately alert. "It sounds like the pony I saw this morning," she cried. "I wonder if it's the same one."

"But yours was called Goldie," said Rosie.

"Goldie, Golddust, same thing really, isn't it?" Alex interrupted. He had already become bored with the conversation.

"Well, she left a phone number," Kate said, handing Jess a scrap of paper.

"Belinda Lang, Colcott, 744-2562. Palomino pony. Golddust." Jess mumbled the words. "Maybe I'll phone her from the tack room once I'm done with Minstrel," she said aloud to no one in particular.

As Jess rubbed Minstrel down absent-mindedly, she thought about Goldie and the man chasing her, and about Belinda too.

"I wonder if it could be the same pony," she reasoned aloud to Minstrel. "A man catching a pony, then this girl saying her pony's lost. I'm sure there must be an explanation for it all." She shrugged her shoulders and gave the pony a final pat. Fingering the scrap of paper in her pocket she walked over to the tack room. But when she got there, Nick was standing at the door and the others were gathered around him.

"I've got some news," Nick said to them all. "Can you take a seat inside?"

Everyone piled in and Nick smiled at the expectant faces turned toward him. Leaning against the messy desk where the rides were scheduled, he folded his arms.

"As you are probably aware," he began. "The Southdown Show is three weeks away."

How could they not be aware? Southdown! It was one of the most prestigious shows in the area – better even than the Benbridge show, where Sandy Lane had done so well in the past. Last year Nick and Sarah had taken the Sandy Lane regulars to Southdown to watch and Jess had loved every minute of it.

"This year at Southdown," Nick continued, ignoring the murmurs of anticipation, "there's going to be a special show jumping event for juniors and I've been invited to enter three riders from Sandy Lane. It's a great honor, but obviously not all of you will be able to participate."

Nick's last words echoed in Jess's head. Nick must choose me to ride. He just *must*, she thought as everyone began talking at once.

"The Southdown Show – cool!"

"It's a *real* horse show."

"Even my mom's heard of it!"

"Which horses will you take?"

"Who will you enter?"

At this last question, the room fell silent again. Who would Nick choose?

"Ah yes." Nick shuffled the papers on the desk in front of him. "The crucial question." He paused for a moment. "Well, there's valuable experience to be gained from taking part in such a prestigious event."

Jess held her breath as Nick continued.

16

"So I think that the riders who would most benefit from this sort of competition right now are Tom, Charlie..."

Tom grinned uncontrollably. Charlie gave a whoop and shot his fist in the air.

"Thank you Charlie," Nick continued dryly, "and Rosie."

Suddenly Jess felt as though she was looking at everyone through the wrong end of a telescope. From far away Nick's voice carried on.

"Tom will ride Chancey, Charlie will be on Napoleon and Rosie will take Pepper," he continued. "Now as I said, the show's in three weeks. Everyone should work hard in lessons until then, whether you're competing or not. I'm sorry that not everyone can compete, but there will be other shows and other chances. You're all excellent riders and I have confidence in all of you." And then Nick was finished. He pushed his chair away from the table and stood up. "Now don't you have jobs to do?" he said, smiling as he left the tack room. And that was that.

"Sandy Lane at the Southdown Show," Kate cried, breaking the silence that followed Nick's departure. "Way to go you three."

"We haven't actually done anything yet," Tom said cheerfully.

"Ah, but you will," said Alex, nudging him in his seat. "You cleaned up at the Benbridge show last year. You can do the same at Southdown."

"You bet we can," Charlie grinned. "The question

is, who'll come first?"

"I'll just be glad to get around the course," Rosie said. "It's a scary thought."

"You'll be brilliant, Rosie," Jess managed at last. "Good job."

Rosie shot her friend an apologetic look. "I don't think I filled Pepper's haynet. Come with me while I do it, Jess?" she asked.

"OK." Jess shrugged, following Rosie out of the tack room. The little piebald looked up at their approach, surprised to see them again so soon.

"I don't know why Nick picked me, Jess," Rosie said softly, drawing back the bolt. "It's a complete surprise."

"Don't be silly, Rosie. You're a really good rider," Jess sighed, picking splinters of wood from Pepper's stall door. "Nick can see that."

"But you wouldn't be scared to jump in a competition, Jess," Rosie wailed. "My legs feel like jelly at the thought of it."

Jess tried to grin. "You'll be fine, Rosie," she croaked at last. "Especially with me there to cheer you on. So – come on Southdown!"

"But not too quickly," Rosie groaned.

* * * * * * * * * * * * * * * * *

A little while later, as Jess wheeled her bicycle across the yard, Nick stopped her with a wave.

"Thanks again for getting the ponies' breakfasts this morning, Jess," he said. "And don't be too disappointed about Southdown. It's a very disciplined event. I'm not sure it's the right competition for you at the moment."

"I know," Jess sighed. "I'm a clumsy rider. I have no poise."

"Nonsense," Nick laughed. "Although I'm glad to see you're being self-critical – that's an important quality for a show jumper. You're a dedicated and instinctive rider Jess. Your chance will come."

"Instinctive," Nick had said. *"Dedicated."* Suddenly everything was all right again. The gray cloud of gloom that had floated into Jess's view lifted and the sun poked through.

"Really?" Jess answered.

"Yes," Nick grinned. "Really."

When Jess returned home later that afternoon she was in a much better mood. She set the table for supper *and* did all the dishes without even being asked.

"Are you feeling OK, Jess?" her mother asked.

It was only as she was undressing for bed and thinking back over the events of the day that a terrible thought struck Jess. In all the excitement she had completely forgotten to call Belinda about the runaway palomino.

"It's too late now," Jess groaned aloud. "I'll have to do it first thing tomorrow. Oh why did I forget?"

Jess crawled underneath her comforter, but it was a long time before she slept. When at last she did, her dreams were disturbed by pictures of the runaway pony jumping a clear round at Southdown. But, try as she might, Jess couldn't see who was riding her...

3

JUMPING LESSON

"This is 744-2562," a mechanical female voice intoned at the end of the line. "I am sorry there is no one here to take your call at the moment, but if you'd like to leave a message we'll get right back to you."

Jess grimaced. She hated answering machines. She twisted the telephone cord between her fingers as she stood in the tack room, Belinda's number on the table in front of her. As the tone sounded she spoke quickly.

"Hello," she said. "I'm trying to reach Belinda. I think I've seen your pony. My name is Jess Adams and I'll be at Sandy Lane Stables all day if you want to talk to me." She replaced the receiver and looked at her watch. Twenty minutes until the next lesson. They were practicing jumping today and all the regulars would be there.

Jess raced over to Minstrel's stable. Storm Cloud stood looking over her door and whinnied as Jess went by. Jess grinned and reached into her pocket for the sugar cube she had saved especially for her.

"Here you go Stormy," she whispered in the pony's gray ear as she gave her the sugar cube. "Don't tell anyone else, or they'll all want one."

Storm Cloud tossed her mane in conspiratorial reply and crunched on the tasty treat.

"See you later," Jess called as she went to get Minstrel ready.

In the stable next door, Rosie was tacking up Pepper.

"I hope the jumps aren't too high today," Rosie said as they led the ponies out of their stables and took them down the drive to the outdoor ring.

"Bring your horses into the middle here," Nick called as they approached. "And I'll hold them while you walk the course."

"This sounds serious," Rosie muttered as she followed Jess through the gate.

Charlie and Tom had just finished inspecting the jumps as Jess and Rosie followed Kate and Alex around. There were eight obstacles in all, starting with some cross poles and ending with a small wall. There was also a low, but nevertheless, difficult, double in the middle.

"They look pretty tough," Rosie said to Jess as they walked back to get Minstrel and Pepper from Nick.

"It's only because Nick has tried to set up a proper course, Rosie," Jess smiled. "We've jumped higher before."

"Right," said Nick. "So what do you think of my course?" He turned to them and smiled. "I was tempted to bring along a bell to ring and a loud speaker to announce each rider as they entered the ring – just like a real show jumping competition."

Everyone groaned.

"Don't worry," Nick continued. "These jumps are no harder than anything you've tried before. I'm confident they shouldn't cause too many problems."

Jess turned to Rosie. "See, what did I tell you?" she smiled encouragingly.

"Piece of cake these jumps," Charlie said in Jess's ear as he rode by on Napoleon.

"OK you guys," Nick called from the ground. "We've got work to do here. Now, I know you're all at varying levels of riding ability, and some of you," he shot a quick glance at Charlie, "may think that this course is too easy. However, there's more to a successful round than just getting over the jumps. It requires planning and preparation if you want to do it swiftly and carefully. There are no short cuts. That's why it's essential to walk the course first. Got it?"

They all nodded vigorously.

"Good," Nick said. "Tom, would you like to test the course for us please?" He winked in Tom's direction.

Tom smiled ruefully and urged Chancey on. The pair jumped swiftly with fluid movement.

"Tom makes it look so easy," Rosie breathed as he

jumped the wall and finished the course with a clean round.

"He's fantastic," Jess agreed.

"Good job, Tom," said Nick. "Now, who wants to go next?"

Before anyone had a chance to answer, Charlie stormed ahead on Napoleon and jumped clear. Jess was just thinking that he looked like a real show jumper, when Nick's words cut across her.

"Not bad Charlie," he said. "Let's have a little more thought and a little less flourish next time please. You almost skidded poor Napoleon on some of those turns. It's important to jump swiftly, but it isn't worth risking your horse by cutting the corners too much."

Charlie reddened and Jess felt a pang of sympathy. She could tell he had been pleased with his round, but Nick's words had brought him down to earth with a bump. For the first time, Jess began to feel a little nervous. If Nick finds fault with Charlie, what's he going to think about my jumping? she wondered.

Rosie took the course next. She wasn't fast but she was steady, popping Pepper over the jumps in a self-contained way. Jess could see why Nick believed Rosie had a chance at Southdown.

"Come on Jess," Nick called as Rosie rode out of the ring. "It's your turn. Take it slowly. Think of your center line and keep the jumps directly in your sight as you approach."

Jess nodded and turned Minstrel toward the first jump. She knew that Nick's course actually wasn't that difficult. She tried to approach the first jump with confidence. Minstrel took it in his stride and Jess began to enjoy herself as she let Minstrel race on. Suddenly the double loomed sooner than she had anticipated.

"I haven't judged the pacing correctly," she muttered to herself as she felt Minstrel alter his stride. She tried to remember Nick's words of advice – *"Think of your center line... keep the jumps in your sight..."*

Crack! Minstrel just clipped the top pole of the second part of the double. It rocked precariously and fell to the ground with a dull thud. Jess's heart plummeted.

"A bit impulsive, Jess," Nick said as she finished. "That's four faults. If it's any consolation, your time was fast."

Jess tried to smile, but she was annoyed with herself. If she had been more careful she would have jumped clean.

"Come on Hector," Alex urged, as he rode him forward. Hector, practically a carthorse at over 16 hands, took the jumps slowly and steadily with a lumbering stride, but they made it.

"Good work, Alex," Nick called. "You did well to push Hector around that course. OK, Kate. It's your turn to jump."

Jess's brain was whirring. I'm the only one to have misjudged the jumps so far, she thought.

She was so wrapped up in herself that she wasn't even watching Kate's round on the little bay pony, Jester. Then...

"Oh!" Rosie gasped and Jess looked up to see Jester running out at the brush.

"Do you know what you did wrong, Kate?" Nick called.

"Yes," Kate answered miserably. "I checked him too early. It was my fault."

"Well, learn from your mistakes," said Nick. "Try that one again."

Kate turned Jester and introduced him again to the jump. Face set in grim determination, she gave the signal just at the right moment, and Jester flew over the brush with inches to spare.

Outside in the lane, after the lesson, Jess swung herself down from Minstrel's saddle. Taking the pony by the reins she led her toward the stables. Rosie came up behind them, leading Pepper and grinning madly.

"You jumped really well, Rosie," Jess said.

"You were faster than me, though," Rosie said in reply. "Oh that was fantastic, Jess. I don't know why I always get so nervous before a lesson. I love it when I'm up there."

The two friends led the ponies up to the stables and began rubbing them down after the sweaty ride.

Alex and Charlie were halfway through their chores as Jess and Rosie tied up Minstrel and Pepper and went to work. Tom had already taken Chancey to his stall and Kate was jumping Jester one last time.

"That was a good lesson," Charlie called. "I thought we all did pretty well. Alex and I were just discussing who would have won the Southdown junior trophy based on today's performance."

Jess groaned. "Don't start getting all competitive, Charlie."

Alex laughed. "Uh oh, looks like you've touched a raw nerve there, Charlie," he grinned. "You should know better than to joke about the Southdown Show with Jess. She's a sensitive little soul you know."

This was almost more than Jess could bear. She *wasn't* upset about Southdown. Not really. But that still didn't give Alex the right to tease her about it. He would have to be taught a lesson. Dipping a dandy brush into the bucket of water, she flicked it at Alex. Water sprayed over Charlie too. Rosie shrieked with laughter at the sight and Jess grinned triumphantly.

"Water fight!" the boys whooped excitedly.

Soon there was water everywhere and the four children were drenched. Water soaked into the hay on the ground and stuck in clumps to their feet. Alex leapt back to avoid another soaking and caught his elbow on a pile of yard brushes stacked in the corner, bringing them clattering down around him.

"Hey what's going on here?" Sarah said firmly as she rounded the corner of the stables. "I hate to interrupt your fun," she said, "but someone is asking for you in the tack room, Jess."

"It must be the Southdown talent scout!" Charlie couldn't help saying.

Before Jess could douse him again, Sarah spoke. "It's a girl actually, about your age Jess. Says her name's Belinda. Something about a missing palomino."

Jess's heart skipped a beat. "Did she have a pony with her?" she asked Sarah eagerly.

"No," Sarah replied. "She's on her own. Come on you guys." Sarah turned to the others. "Let's get this mess cleaned up now."

Jess glanced at Rosie. "I wonder if Belinda's found Goldie yet?" she said.

"Go and find out," Rosie urged. "I'll finish up here, don't worry."

Jess gave her friend a grateful wave and raced toward the tack room. There, waiting outside the door, was a tall, slim girl. She stood staring into the middle distance. She wore soft beige britches and a white shirt. Jess was suddenly horribly aware of her own rather disheveled appearance. Her hair lay in wet rats' tails from the soaking she had been given, and hay stuck to her T-shirt in clumps. Slowly she approached the girl with none of the confidence she had mustered the morning she had caught the palomino.

"H-Hello," she stammered. "I'm Jess. Are you Belinda?"

The girl turned her gaze toward Jess and stared at her for a few moments. Jess shifted from one foot to the other.

"That's right," Belinda said at last. "You said on the phone that you'd seen Golddust."

On closer inspection, Jess saw that Belinda's face

was pinched and white.

"Well, I think it must have been her. A palomino mare came racing into the stable grounds yesterday morning," Jess explained. "She was about 14 hands. She had the most beautiful white-gold mane and a long, flowing tail."

"That sounds like Golddust," Belinda said quickly. "I went to her field at seven yesterday morning, like I always do, and she wasn't there. So is she here now?" Belinda asked. "Did you catch her?"

"Yes, I caught her," Jess began slowly. "But she isn't here. There was a man chasing her."

"A man? What man?" Belinda suddenly looked panic-stricken.

"Um," Jess stammered. "This man who was running after Golddust... only he called her Goldie. He said she was a devil to catch... he said Goldie was his daughter's pony..." Jess's words came out in staccato breaths.

Belinda's face looked blank with amazement at what Jess was saying and she started to stammer. "That's impossible," she said. "I don't have a father... he's dead."

Jess opened her mouth to say something, but before she could get the words out, Belinda spoke.

"It's obvious," she cried, and in that moment Jess realized the awful truth. "Golddust hasn't run away at all," Belinda wailed. "She's been stolen!"

4

JESS IS SORRY

Jess sat at the desk in the tack room, her head in her hands. "It all makes sense now. That man must have been actually stealing Golddust! And I helped him. What an idiot I am. Oh Belinda, I'm so sorry." Belinda stood, fiddling with Storm Cloud's bridle, which was hanging from a peg on the wall. Now she turned to Jess and shrugged sadly.

"Look, you wouldn't have known," she began. "You didn't do it on purpose."

Jess looked up and managed a smile. "You're being very nice about all this," she said. "It's making me feel even worse. I'd be furious, if I were you."

Belinda sighed. "What's the point?" she reasoned. "Golddust is gone, and there's nothing we can do about it."

At that moment Sarah appeared at the door of the

tack room, followed closely by Rosie. Sarah smiled encouragingly at Jess.

"Rosie's just been telling me about yesterday morning and the palomino pony," she said.

Jess's heart sank. Of course, Sarah didn't know yet that Golddust was stolen. And nor did Rosie. Quickly Jess explained what had happened. When she had finished, Rosie gasped in dismay. "Oh, Jess, that man must have been a thief! But how did he know the pony's name?"

"I suppose Goldie is just as obvious a name for a palomino as Golddust," said Belinda. "Not a very imaginative choice, I know, but it does describe her exactly."

"Look, I think it would be a good idea to go to the police about all this," said Sarah. Her voice was reassuring and capable. "You must give a statement Jess. And a description of the man you saw, if you can. It might help them find Belinda's pony sooner."

The police! Jess swallowed hard.

"Do you want me to come with you for moral support?" Sarah asked. "I could drive you in the Bronco if you like. I've got some spare time now."

Jess nodded gratefully. If she had to go to the police, she would rather Sarah came with her.

"Yes please," she replied.

"What about you, Belinda?" Sarah said gently. "Would you like to come with us?"

Belinda shook her head. "They already know

Golddust is missing," she explained. "I went to the police station earlier today. My mom took me. They had no news of course. There's no point in me going back there again."

"Well, if you'd rather stay here and wait until we come back, I understand," said Sarah.

Jess didn't understand at all. If Golddust was *her* pony she imagined she'd be wanting to check the police station every five minutes for news.

"I'll stay with you if you like, Belinda," Rosie looked hesitantly at Belinda. "I think there's some lemonade in the fridge. Would you like some?"

Belinda shrugged her shoulders. "All right," she said.

Jess shot Rosie a look of thanks and followed Sarah to the Bronco.

When they arrived, Jess found that giving a statement to the police wasn't actually too difficult. She had to go over the whole morning in tiny detail.

"You will find Golddust won't you?" Jess asked, concerned. "You will catch the thief."

"Well, we'll do our best," the friendly desk sergeant assured her. "But it's not always that easy."

"What do you think he might have done with Golddust?" Jess asked.

The sergeant shrugged. "Well, he could be planning to sell her at auction. He could have a private buyer..."

Jess sat hunched miserably in the Bronco on the short drive back to Sandy Lane.

"These things happen, Jess," Sarah said to her. "It's why we have to be extra-cautious about security. I'm afraid ponies are easy targets."

The Bronco crunched into the driveway of the stable and Jess got out. While Sarah parked outside the house, Jess walked back to the tack room. Rosie was waiting eagerly for her, but there was no sign of Belinda.

"How did it go?" Rosie asked.

"Oh, all right I suppose," Jess replied, sinking down into the old wicker chair in the corner of the room. "The police aren't exactly rushing around looking for clues with dogs and magnifying glasses."

Rosie laughed. "Well I guess they know what they're doing," she said.

"Where's Belinda?" Jess asked abruptly.

"She's gone home," Rosie replied.

"Gone home?" Jess was incredulous. "Why? If *my* pony was missing I'd be out there looking for it, not sitting at home. Honestly, she hardly seemed angry or upset. *I* feel really worried and nervous for Golddust and she isn't even my pony!"

"I think Belinda *is* upset." Rosie paused as she tried to explain. "She's just not showing it the way you would. Listen to this – she told me her dad died six months ago and she's just moved to Colcott where she doesn't know anybody and now her pony's been stolen. If that had happened to me I'd probably lock myself in my bedroom and bawl my eyes out for months."

Jess thought about what Rosie had said and was

silent for a moment. She hadn't thought of it like that.

"Maybe, Rosie," Jess sighed. Then she perked up. "So it's a good thing she's met us!" she cried.

"Uh oh, why's that?" Rosie said slowly.

"Well, it's obvious really," Jess replied. "Golddust is out there somewhere, Rosie, and *we're* going to find her."

"We?" Rosie croaked.

"Yes! It's partly my fault Golddust is missing anyway. So it's the least I can do," Jess continued. "Just you wait, Rosie. Belinda won't be miserable for much longer. Not with Jess Adams and Rosie Edwards on Golddust's trail!"

5

NEAR DISASTER

The next day was Monday and Jess was at the stables again. She was eager to start searching for Golddust right away. The local paper had been lying around in the tack room and Jess wanted to check it for details of horse sales. She passed Storm Cloud's stall on the way. The beautiful gray was looking out over the top of the half door. Jess gave her an affectionate pat.

"Hello Stormy," she said. "You're looking lovely today."

"Jess," Nick called, walking across the yard. "I've got a job for you. Sarah's at the tack shop and I have to go to the feed store. Someone's coming for a ride in twenty minutes. Could you tack up Minstrel?"

"Yes, of course," said Jess. "Who's riding?"

"A new girl, called Petronella Slater."

"Has she ridden before?" Jess asked.

"Yes, but not here," Nick replied. "She's trying out Sandy Lane for the first time, and if she likes it, I hope she'll come back. We need the business," he muttered, almost to himself. "Anyway, I spoke to her father on the phone. Actually I know him vaguely. He seems to think Petronella's a good rider. He's going to buy her a pony of her own pretty soon."

"Lucky her," Jess sighed.

Nick laughed sympathetically. "Well, he wants Petronella to ride for a while at Sandy Lane before she takes on that responsibility anyway."

"Who'll be taking her out?" Jess asked.

"Tom," Nick answered. "He should be here any minute." Nick climbed into his truck and drove away.

"See you later," Jess called as she headed for the tack room. No one else had arrived for the day. Jess reached up to get Minstrel's saddle from its hook. Glancing to the left, she realized that Chancey's tack was still in its place. Tom was running late. That wasn't like him. He was normally very reliable and always on time. For a fleeting moment Jess was concerned. But at that moment the tack room door swung open and Tom stumbled inside.

"There you are," Jess said. "I was beginning to worry. Did you know you've got a trail ride in about ten minutes' time? I was just about to tack up Minstrel. You're taking out someone called Petronella Slater. What a name!"

Jess stopped abruptly as she caught sight of Tom's

face. He was ghostly white and could hardly stand straight.

"Are you all right Tom?" she asked. "You look awful."

"I'm not sure." Tom collapsed heavily into the wicker chair. "I feel terrible. I was a little sick when I woke up this morning. I've just cycled here and my stomach's killing me. I feel all hot and shaky."

"Oh poor you," Jess sympathised. "Perhaps you have the flu."

"Ow ow ow," Tom groaned. "No, it feels worse than that. I don't think I can take that ride out, Jess. I can hardly stand straight. Where's Nick?"

"He's gone to get some feed. And Sarah's at the tack shop. What are we going to do Tom? It's too late to cancel this girl."

"Well, we'll just have to explain and ask her to come back another day," Tom said.

"Or I could take her out!" Jess cried impulsively. "I could ride another horse. Hector maybe. He's really reliable. It'd be a lot better than having to turn her away. It would be bad for business. That's what Nick would say."

Tom managed a half smile, despite his obvious pain. "Well," he began. "Nick has let you lead trail rides before, hasn't he?"

"Yes, I've done it twice," Jess replied proudly.

Tom seemed to make up his mind quickly. "Go ahead then," he said. "You've got two ponies to tack up in under ten minutes!"

"OK," Jess smiled happily. She wanted a chance to prove she was capable. Everyone had heard the story of Golddust by now and how she had practically handed the pony over to a thief. She had been expecting some teasing about it, especially from Charlie. But no one had said anything. Still, she was determined to make everyone, especially Tom and Nick, see she wasn't a complete idiot. She would take the trail ride and show them how responsible and competent she really was.

"I'll come back for Hector's things in a minute," she called to Tom. But Tom was silent, his face pinched with pain.

Jess raced to the stable. She had just finished Minstrel and was on her way back for Hector's tack when a shiny white Jeep pulled into the yard. A haughty looking girl in immaculate fawn britches stepped out. In her hand she held a black riding crop. She was about Jess's age. A tall man got out from the driver's side. The girl gave the stable grounds an imperious once over as the man turned a questioning gaze toward Jess.

"I booked a ride for my daughter," he began.

"It's a hack Daddy," the girl hissed loudly. "You booked a hack – that's how they say it in *England*."

"Ah yes, I did indeed," the man agreed.

What a snob this girl is, Jess thought. Aloud she said "Are you Petronella Slater?"

"Yes I am," the girl replied.

"Right. Well, hello," Jess continued. "I'm Jess

Adams, and I'll be taking you out today. And this," she said turning to Minstrel, "is the pony you'll be riding, Minstrel."

Petronella looked scornfully at the pony.

"Kind of a nag, isn't she? She doesn't look very fast."

"She's a he, actually." Jess flushed angrily. Did this girl really know anything about riding? How dare she call Minstrel a nag? Jess bit her tongue. It wouldn't be a good idea to upset a new rider.

"He loves galloping," she said through gritted teeth. But Petronella wasn't impressed.

"No, he won't do at all," she said, waving her riding crop dismissively. "Far too ordinary. Ah, now that's the kind of thing I should be riding."

Jess turned to where Petronella was pointing – right at Storm Cloud, who was hanging her head over her stall door as usual.

"Oh I'm sorry," Jess said quickly, jumping to defend the gray pony. "That's Storm Cloud. No one's allowed to take her out unless they've been riding here a while. She's part-Arab and really precious. She's also sort of flighty and a little unpredictable."

"Exactly what I'm looking for," said Petronella. "I *am* an experienced rider you know. Obviously no one explained that to you." She turned to the man with her. "Daddy, tell the girl I can ride her."

"Well," Mr. Slater began, turning to Jess. "That horse..."

"Pony," Jess muttered.

"Ah, yes, pony. She does look nice. So what's the problem?" he asked. "Is Nick Brooks around? I spoke to him on the phone."

"No, he's not." Jess shifted uncomfortably. The situation was slipping away from her and she wasn't sure what to do.

"Daddy, if you're going to make me ride at these stables before I'm allowed to have my own pony, I should be allowed to ride who I want," Petronella interrupted peevishly.

"All right my Pet," Mr. Slater soothed, and Jess began to feel sick.

"Now look here young lady," he said, addressing himself firmly to Jess. "Why don't you let Petronella ride that Storm Cloud creature? Don't worry, I'll square it with Nick when he comes back. We're old friends, you know, so it will be all right. And I *am* paying for this after all."

Jess was furious, but managed to bite her tongue. Well, if Petronella and her dad wouldn't listen to her advice, that was their problem. Handing Minstrel's reins to Petronella, she ran to the tack room to get Storm Cloud's things. For a fleeting moment Jess wondered if what she was doing was such a good idea. But Jess was determined to prove she could handle it on her own and Mr. Slater had been so insistent, she couldn't back down now.

Hurrying back to Storm Cloud's stall, she tacked her up and led the little pony out. Storm Cloud was excited to be going out and Petronella had a hard time mounting the pony, who skipped and pirouetted around the yard.

"See you later, Daddy," Petronella called and then she was off down the lane at a brisk walk. Jess winced as Petronella sawed furiously on the reins and waved her crop dangerously high around the pony's eyes. Storm Cloud tossed her neck as she fought for control of her head. Jess urged Minstrel into a lively trot and followed them out of the stable grounds.

"She's raring to go," Petronella called over her shoulder.

Jess nudged Minstrel on and overtook Petronella, leading them along the bumpy coastal track toward the lighthouse where Sarah had taken them only a few days before.

"There are some good places for a gallop around here," she called back to Petronella.

To the right of them the grass stretched away invitingly, and Jess could feel that Minstrel was eager for a race. Storm Cloud was positively foaming at the mouth and the more she pulled, the tighter Petronella tugged at the reins, until poor Stormy's ears were almost touching the girl's scornfully turned up nose. Jess winced.

"Perhaps you should give her a little more rein," she said. "And stop waving that crop. She'd probably calm down a little."

"Nonsense," Petronella sneered. "You have to show them who's boss. Besides, who wants to ride a calm pony? This is far more exciting. Come on, let's go!"

And with that, she gave Storm Cloud a resounding whack with the crop. For a fraction of a second Storm Cloud seemed to hover in midair, almost stunned by the pain. And then she shot off and bolted across the field. Petronella pulled desperately on the reins, but it was too late. She had lost control.

"You stupid girl," Jess cried in dismay and disbelief.

For a moment Jess watched helplessly as the fragile gray careened across the fields at breakneck speed. Swerving round to the left, she pounded on toward Larkfield Copse. Jess gasped as the pony gathered pace. She was headed straight for the trees and Petronella couldn't turn her. Jess went cold as she thought of the low-hanging branches.

Now Jess urged Minstrel on into a gallop. The little pony didn't need much encouragement and he raced off, mane and tail flying in the breeze.

Ahead, Petronella screamed loudly and shut her eyes tight with terror. Minstrel's pounding hooves rang in Jess's ears and her eyes streamed with water as the wind bit into her face. Faster and faster Minstrel raced. Storm Cloud was well in front, but she was weaving from side to side. Jess concentrated on keeping Minstrel in a straight line, and soon they were gaining on them. All the time the low-hanging branches of Larkfield Copse loomed nearer.

The sweat rose on Minstrel's neck, and still Jess urged him on. Now at last they were galloping alongside Storm Cloud. They were only feet away from the trees. Petronella had dropped Storm Cloud's reins, and they were hanging loosely as she clung to his mane. Minstrel and Storm Cloud were neck and neck. With the utmost effort, Jess leaned over as far as she dared and grabbed Storm Cloud's reins. It seemed like the only thing to do. She pulled hard and brought Storm Cloud's head around to the left, turning Minstrel at just the same time.

Storm Cloud seemed surprised that someone had taken charge and followed immediately. But Petronella stayed where she was and, as Storm Cloud and Minstrel changed direction, Petronella went flying forward, sailing over Storm Cloud's neck. She landed with a thump in a patch of mud at the edge of the trees.

Jess brought Minstrel to a stop alongside the field and Storm Cloud followed obediently. As she gathered up Storm Cloud's reins, the little gray sprang back nervously. Her nostrils quivered and her heaving flanks were covered in foam and sweat.

"Whoa there, Stormy," Jess cooed softly as she jumped out of the saddle. "You're all right now."

Slowly, Storm Cloud calmed down. She listened intently to Jess and nuzzled her nose wearily into Jess's shoulder. Positioning herself between the two ponies, Jess looked over to Petronella.

"Are you all right?" she called.

"No, of course I'm not all right," Petronella howled, brushing the dirt from the seat of her pants. "That animal is dangerous. She shouldn't be allowed out."

Jess was furious. "You insisted on riding her," she couldn't help saying. "Couldn't you see that she was worked up already? The last thing she needed was a beating from a crop to get her going."

"How... how dare you," Petronella retorted. "*You're* the one to blame. You and this stupid horse. I wasn't properly supervised! I'm going to report you to... to Nick Brooks."

"What's going on here?" a familiar voice interrupted.

Jess spun around. Nick! The Bronco was parked at an angle in the field and Nick was striding toward them. Jess's relief at his reassuring presence soon gave way to trepidation at the thought of what he might say.

"I was worried when I got back to the stables and found that Storm Cloud was missing and Chancey was still in his stall. What happened? Where's Tom?"

Quickly Jess explained everything – Tom's illness, Petronella's insistence on riding Storm Cloud and Jess's own part in it all.

Nick looked sternly at her and took a deep breath. "Well, we'll talk about this later, Jess," he said. "Are you OK?" he asked, turning to face Petronella. "Can you stand up?"

Petronella got shakily to her feet. She swayed a little as she stood up and put a hand to her head. Nick held out a steadying hand. "Take it slowly now," he said.

"I'm all right," Petronella said fiercely. Her face was determined, but Jess saw tears in her eyes.

"I'll take you back in the truck," Nick said gently. "Jess can lead Minstrel and Storm Cloud."

"No!" Petronella cried. Then, seeing Nick's startled face she tried to explain. "I mean... I can't let my father see me like this. You won't tell him?" She looked at Nick despairingly.

"Well, I don't know..." Nick began. Petronella pleaded again.

"If he hears about this he'll never let me have my own pony," she continued. "Not a really good one, anyway. He'll get me some safe, plodding old thing."

Jess looked on in amazement and Nick shook his head slowly. "You can't fool him that you're a better rider than you are, Petronella," he said. "Look, why don't you continue to have a few lessons at Sandy Lane before you get your pony? I think you'd find it a big help. Even the best riders still have lessons," he added hastily as Petronella tried to speak. "And the more experience you have, the more you'll enjoy having your own pony."

"Well..." Petronella hesitated. "If I come and ride at Sandy Lane, will you promise not to tell my father what's happened today?"

Jess let out a gasp of astonishment. What nerve! Imagine talking to Nick like that! Even Nick seemed a little taken aback, for it was a while before he spoke. When he did, his voice was serious.

"I don't make bargains, Petronella," he said sternly. "And I do think you need some more practice. Now, do you think you're up to riding Minstrel back, under

Jess's supervision?" Petronella nodded quickly.

"OK. Good girl," said Nick. "Jess." He turned to her. "I think it's best if you ride Storm Cloud back to the stables, and I'd like to talk to you once you've untacked the ponies."

He turned on his heel and walked back to his truck. Jess looked on in astonishment and it was a moment before she came to her senses. Nick had told her to ride Storm Cloud. Not in the school, not around the stable grounds, but out in the open – and after Storm Cloud had bolted too. For a moment, she didn't even mind Nick's parting shot *I'd like to talk to you*. Right now all that mattered was Storm Cloud.

She gathered up the reins and mounted. "Walk on," she said softly, and Storm Cloud moved forward.

Jess glanced back. Petronella followed on behind. She was calmer now, and Jess noted that she really wasn't such a bad rider when she wasn't showing off.

Jess turned to look ahead again. Storm Cloud's step was quick and eager as Jess kept a light but steadying control on the rein. She longed to have a gallop. She knew Storm Cloud would go like the wind, but she stopped herself.

"I'd better not try anything risky, or Nick will never trust me again. Come on Stormy," she murmured. "Let's go home."

6

A TURN OF EVENTS

"What exactly was wrong with Tom then?" Nick asked, in a stern voice. "You said he was sick."

"Yes, he felt sick," Jess answered quietly. "So I said I'd take Petronella out."

Jess stood in the kitchen of Nick and Sarah's house. She traced a small circle in the cracked red linoleum with the toe of her boot and stared at her feet. Nick stood with his back to the sink, leaning against it, his arms folded. He looked down at Jess and continued.

"I've given you permission to take out trail rides before Jess, but in this instance I knew Tom was the best person for the job. He's much more experienced than you are, I'm afraid."

Jess swallowed hard and tried to hold back the tears.

"And I think you know Storm Cloud wasn't a good

choice for Petronella, either," Nick went on.

Jess nodded miserably. "I'm sorry Nick. I just thought I was doing the right thing. And I did try to warn Petronella, but Mr. Slater said he knew you and that it would be all right."

"I don't know him *that* well," Nick continued. "But I appreciate how difficult it must be to go against an adult's wishes."

"I'm sorry," Jess croaked again.

"Anyway, I was impressed with the way you handled Storm Cloud, Jess. You remained calm and collected in the face of a potentially dangerous situation. Good job." Jess blushed furiously.

"Right, that's the lecture over with. Back to the stables." Nick gestured with a nod towards the door. "It must be lunch time."

Jess gave a grateful wave and hurried to the tack room but there was no one there. She settled down by herself to eat her lunch. As she munched, Jess replayed the ride on Storm Cloud over and over in her mind.

Sandwich in one hand, she spread the local paper out on her lap and hunched over the crumpled page, scanning the list of open air markets.

"I'll show everybody I can do something right," she said aloud. "Now where are we? Benbridge Women's Institute Floral Display... April 14th-21st. St. Olaf's Parish Church." She ran her finger down the small black lettering, brushing aside crumbs. "Livestock day at Bucknell Pig Farm."

And then she found what she was looking for – "The

Ash Hill Horse Sale. 2nd Thursday of every month. Horses and ponies for sale at auction. 10 am at Ash Hill Showground."

Jess did some rapid calculating. It was Monday the 7th today – the second Monday of the month – so the sale was in three days'.

"Caught you!" A voice shouted in her ear. Jess jumped up, startled, and the paper slid to the floor.

"Looking for Golddust already I see," Rosie grinned.

"Yes, but something else has happened, Rosie. I've just had the most awful morning," Jess began, thinking back over the ride with Petronella.

"Another one?" Rosie grinned. "What was it this time? More runaway ponies? International horse thieves?"

Jess laughed and began to tell Rosie about what happened.

"Petronella Slater?" Rosie wrinkled up her nose as Jess finished her explanation. "I've never heard of her... she's not at our school, that's for sure."

"Thank goodness," Jess said heartily. She picked up the paper and stabbed at it with her forefinger. "Anyway, we've got more important things to think about, Rosie. There's a sale at Ash Hill in three days. It only happens once a month so the man who stole Golddust can't have been there yet."

"That's where Nick bought Storm Cloud," said Rosie.

"Exactly," Jess replied. "So that's a good omen." She smiled cheerfully and if she had been about to say more, her words were halted by the arrival of Alex and Kate. They came bounding into the tack room arguing with each other as usual. Charlie followed close behind and greeted everyone with a casual wave. Now all the regulars were here.

"Has anyone seen Tom?" she asked.

They all shook their heads.

"Not yet," Alex said. "We've got a jumping lesson though, so he should be here soon."

"I'm sorry, but I'm afraid he won't be." Sarah appeared on the step of the tack room, a hand held up for silence. Her face was solemn. "I've got some bad news. Tom's mother called a little while ago. He's been taken to the hospital," she went on.

"Hospital?" Alex gasped. "What's wrong?"

"They're not sure at the moment, which is why he's staying there," Sarah replied. "His mother said he had stomach pains this morning, but he seemed well enough to ride his bike into Sandy Lane. You saw him, didn't you Jess?"

Jess nodded quickly. "He looked awful."

"Well he managed to ride home again, but he was in a lot of pain," Sarah explained. "He insisted his mother phone us. He was afraid Chancey might be neglected if he didn't show up for his lesson."

"Typical Tom." Alex tried to laugh, but Jess could see he was worried.

"Now, look, he wouldn't want you to worry," said Sarah. "And he's in the best place. As soon as I have any more news I'll let you know. Anyway, I'm going to exercise Chancey now. And you've all got a jumping

50

lesson, haven't you?"

Everyone stood around dumbstruck, until Sarah snapped them out of their trances.

"Get a move on then," she called. "Nick's waiting."

"Yes, come on everyone," said Charlie. "Buck up. Worrying isn't going to win us any Southdown trophies," he said gruffly. "I'm going to go tack up Napoleon."

* * * * * * * * * * * * * * * * *

"I wish we knew what was wrong with Tom," Alex groaned as the lesson came to an end. It had been a subdued hour. They had all jumped well, but without enthusiasm. Jess had cleared the course, but unspectacularly and with all her thoughts on Tom.

"Perhaps we should all go to the hospital, now," Kate said. "And not leave until we find out if Tom's going to be OK."

"Don't be silly, Kate," said Charlie. "Tom's mother is bound to call again when there's any more news."

"Let's hang around the stables for a while then," Rosie said when they had fed and groomed the ponies. "We should wait for news."

"OK," Jess agreed as they flopped down on some hay bales behind the big barn. "And to take our minds off things, we can make plans for finding Golddust. Apart from going to Ash Hill, I thought we should put posters up. We could try farriers and vets, local shows, that kind of thing. I know Belinda's already started on asking at riding stables – not that there are many around here. But there's much more we can do..."

Rosie stopped Jess with a laugh. "Whoa, slow down Jess," she cried. "Aren't you forgetting something?"

"What?" Jess asked eagerly. "Horse sales, posters... what should I have remembered?"

"Belinda!" Rosie reminded her. "Shouldn't she be involved as well? After all, Golddust is her pony. Maybe she's had the same ideas as you."

"Oh yes," Jess paused. "Maybe Belinda would start to feel happier if she really started to search for Golddust too."

"And if she knew we wanted to help she might feel a little better," Rosie pointed out.

"You're right, Rosie," Jess said. "I'll phone her now and tell her we'll help."

"Take it slowly, Jess," said Rosie. "You don't want to frighten her off. You can be a little overwhelming sometimes."

"I know," Jess smiled as Kate raced toward them.

"Come quickly!" Kate cried. "Sarah's got news about Tom. She's going to tell us all in the tack room."

Jess and Rosie raced with Kate to the tack room. Charlie and Alex were already there and Sarah began to speak.

"It's appendicitis," she announced. "Tom's going

to have an operation this afternoon. He'll be in the hospital for several days," she went on. "But it will take a lot longer than that before he is completely better."

"When will he be able to ride again?" Alex asked.

"Not for a while I guess," said Sarah. "A month or so, maybe more."

"So he'll miss Southdown?" Charlie said.

"It looks like it," Sarah replied.

"Poor Tom," said Rosie.

"Poor Chancey," said Jess.

* * * * * * * * * * * * * * * *

Jess was still thinking about Tom later that evening as she rode her bike through Colcott and on to the new houses at the edge of town. She was going to see Belinda.

Jess had called earlier and arranged to come over. Belinda had been hesitant on the phone, but Jess sensed a hint of curiosity in her voice. Jess was pretty excited.

In her mind, she had already found Golddust and was receiving Belinda's heart-felt thanks. This thought pleased Jess so much that it carried her swiftly along the road and right past Belinda's house. Turning her bike sharply she pedaled back and checked the house number. 34 Archway Avenue. This was it. The grassy front yard was encircled by a low hedge, and a small stone statue of a dancing horse stood guard on the front step.

"You must be Jess," Belinda's mother said as she opened the door. "Come in." She called up the stairs. "Belinda... you have a visitor!"

Belinda appeared on the top step. She was wearing jeans and a dark blue sweater and her hair was pulled back in a ponytail. She gave Jess a half smile. "I suppose the police didn't have any news about Golddust?" she said.

"No, sorry," Jess shook her head.

Belinda shrugged. "Oh well, you can come up to my room, if you like." She disappeared through a door at the top of the stairs.

"See you later, Jess," Belinda's mother smiled as Jess followed Belinda to her bedroom a little doubtfully.

When Jess stepped into the room, she relaxed immediately. Belinda's bedroom walls were plastered with posters and pictures. Horses and ponies of all shapes and sizes stared down at Jess. There were ribbons of all colors, but mainly blue, Jess noticed enviously.

"I won those with Golddust," Belinda said, following Jess's eye to the ribbons. "She's a really good showjumper."

"Lucky you," Jess said.

"Do you ride at Sandy Lane regularly then?" Belinda said.

"Yes," Jess replied eagerly. "I don't have my own pony or anything, but the Sandy Lane ponies are really nice. Especially Storm Cloud. She's my favorite."

"Is that the little gray one?" Belinda asked, Jess's enthusiasm igniting a flicker of curiosity.

"Yes," Jess said in surprise. "How did you know?"

Belinda smiled again. "Just a guess. I noticed her when I came to the stables yesterday..." She stopped suddenly and looked sad again.

"Belinda," Jess said quickly. "I've got something to tell you. Rosie and I want to help you look for Golddust. We thought we could put up stolen notices and look around horse sales. There's one on Thursday..." She stopped and thought for a moment. "If you want our help, that is," she finished.

Belinda was quiet but her eyes were shining.

"Would you really help me?" she cried at last. "Oh thank you!" And then she was off. She started telling Jess what had happened and didn't pause for a breath. Jess sat and listened and didn't interrupt. She heard how Belinda's mother had had to look for a job after Belinda's father died. She had finally found one in Colcott and they'd had to move. And how Belinda was going to be starting at a new school after Easter.

Belinda told Jess how she had been keeping Golddust in a field on the edge of town for the time being until her mother earned enough to pay for stabling. She told her how she had begun to look for Golddust. And finally Belinda told Jess how upset she had felt when she had gone to Sandy Lane Stables and seen how friendly everyone was, and how she had felt very alone.

"But you're not alone now," Jess cried. "You've got Rosie and me! And we've got this horse sale to go to on Thursday."

"You're right, Jess," Belinda agreed happily. "Oh wouldn't it be wonderful if we found Golddust there?"

"Yes, it would," Jess smiled and looked around at Belinda's lovely horsy room. "Hey!" she exclaimed, pointing to a color snapshot of a girl and a pony perched on Belinda's book shelf. "Is that you? Can I have a look at it?"

"Of course." Belinda took the photo down and gave it a quick dust with her elbow. "It's me and Golddust at the novice jumping at Benbridge last summer."

"The Benbridge show?" Jess exclaimed. "How fantastic... Tom jumped there last year too. He won the open jumping," she said. She looked down at the photo in her hands. She looked and then she looked again.

"Hey, hang on a minute," Jess said, her voice tightening.

"What's the matter?" said Belinda.

But Jess hardly heard it. All of her earlier optimism vanished in an instant, like a light being switched off. When she spoke her voice didn't sound like her own.

"But Belinda... this isn't Golddust!" she mumbled.

"Of course it's Golddust," Belinda laughed. "I should know. She is my pony. "

"No, I don't mean that, I mean..." Jess swallowed hard and then the words came spilling out. "I mean.. this isn't the same pony I saw at Sandy Lane the other morning. This isn't the pony I helped to catch!"

7

ASH HILL HORSE SALE

"It was awful, Rosie." Jess walked along beside her friend, telling her about the visit to Belinda's house. It was Thursday morning, the day of the Ash Hill sale, and the pair were on their way to the bus stop to meet Belinda. It was the first time they had been properly together since Monday. On Tuesday and Wednesday, Jess's mother had put her foot down and reminded Jess of her other responsibilities. And when her mother was in one of her organizing moods it was, Jess knew, best to obey her. Especially since she wanted to visit Tom in the hospital that afternoon too.

Nick had caught Jess yesterday morning as she was leaving Sandy Lane and told her that Tom wanted her to go and see him in the hospital. Nick was rather mysterious about it, but was gone before Jess could ask any more.

Now Jess filled Rosie in about what had happened at Belinda's house.

"There I was looking at this photo of Golddust and I could see it wasn't the same pony I helped to catch the other morning," she explained. "The palomino *I* saw was pure gold, but I could see from the photo that Golddust has a circle of white hair on her forehead."

"So what did Belinda say?" Rosie was curious.

"She asked me if I was sure and then she just sat there very quietly and didn't really say much. Which made me feel pretty miserable. I thought I could help Belinda find Golddust. Now Belinda has no idea if Golddust has been stolen, has run away, or is lying dead in a ditch somewhere."

"Well at least you know it's not your fault Golddust has disappeared, but what a mystery," Rosie said. "I wonder what happened to the palomino pony *you* saw then. I wonder where it came from."

"I wish I knew," Jess replied. "I went to the police station again this morning... on my own this time. I rode my bike all the way there. And I told them that I made a mistake... that I hadn't seen Belinda's pony after all."

"What did they say?"

"I saw a different policeman this time. He didn't say much, but he raised his eyebrows a lot and shook his head and wrote everything down in a big book and asked me to sign my name. Oh Rosie, is all this pointless? Going to Ash Hill, I mean... trying to help

Belinda find Golddust."

"We said we'd help her look, so we have to," Rosie reasoned. "Watch out, here's Belinda now," she said, seeing the tall girl waiting at the bus stop.

"Hello," Belinda said quietly.

"Hi," Rosie said. "Jess has just been telling me about Golddust not being Golddust. It's really weird."

"I know?" Belinda said as the bus appeared and they clambered aboard. "Strange that two palominos should be running loose on the same day."

Rosie didn't know what to say. They rode in silence for the rest of the way. Jess reached up to ring the bell and the bus shuddered and stopped. The doors swished open and the three girls jumped off. They followed a steady stream of cars and trailers along the road until they came to a turn and a sign in a field that said *Ash Hill Horse Sale.*

They weaved their way through the crowd until they came to the group of horses and ponies up for auction.

"OK, let's be logical about this," said Rosie as she bought a sale catalog. "Are there any ponies that match Golddust's description?"

Jess thumbed through the auction catalog. "If Golddust is here, she'll be a late entry," she reasoned. "After all, there hasn't been much time between her being stolen and this sale."

"That's true," Rosie agreed. "The late additions are on this slip of paper at the back. Look."

There weren't many, but there was still plenty to read.

"Here we go," said Jess, reading aloud.

"Lot forty-two. Palomino pony. 13.2 hands without shoes. Fully warranted."

"Hmm. A little small, but worth a look."

Belinda peered over her shoulder. "Here's another one. Lot fifty-five. Palomino show pony. 14.2 hands. Rising five. Some blemishes, but sound."

"They don't make that one sound very attractive. Still, we can't afford to miss it. It's about the right height." She turned the page. "Lot sixty-six. Registered palomino. Show jumper. 14 hands without shoes. Ideal jumper."

"Hmm, that sounds promising," Rosie joined in. "Any more?"

Jess thumbed through the rest of the catalog and shook her head. "No, that's it. Not many to choose from."

"Good," said Rosie. "That means we can check them out quickly."

"How should we do it? Should we wait for their numbers to be called?" Belinda asked.

"Maybe we should go and have a look at them now," Rosie suggested. "Pretend we're interested buyers."

"What, three girls with no more than a bus fare back between us?" Jess was suddenly hesitant. For a fleeting moment she wondered if this was such a good idea after all. Then she saw Belinda's face, and she knew they had to carry on.

"It's the only choice we have," Rosie said firmly.

"Should we go together or split up?"

"Together, definitely," Belinda said.

As they were faced with row upon row of sad and neglected horses, Jess felt less and less cheerful. There were good ponies of course – the ones destined for riding stables and some for a lucky handful of children who would leave with their very own pony. Jess looked longingly at these fit and healthy animals. At the same time, there was another pony who kept calling for her attention. The runaway palomino she had seen the other morning at Sandy Lane. 'Goldie,' that man had called her. Where was that pony now?

"Lot forty-two," said Rosie. "Here it is." They drew to a halt beside a pony tethered to a pole. Belinda gave one look at the little pony and shook her head.

"Nope. This isn't her."

"That's not even a palomino," said Jess when they came to lot fifty-five. "It's a dun. Definitely a dun."

"That must have been the one with blemishes?" Rosie said. "Maybe they were trying to compensate by choosing a pretty color for her."

Lot sixty-six was beautiful. A really gentle palomino with kind eyes. "But it's not Golddust," Belinda sighed. She began to look defeated and Jess felt despondent.

"Come on," Rosie said. "I've got a packed lunch. Let's share it."

Slowly they walked away from the ponies and flopped down as they reached a small group of trees.

"Cheese and tomato or ham?" Rosie said, offering

the sandwiches to the others.

"Cheese," said Jess. "Actually, I'd better eat this pretty quickly," she cried, glancing at her watch. "I've got to go and see Tom this afternoon. I have to get a move on."

* * * * * * * * * * * * * * * *

"You look a bit green, Tom."

"Thanks a lot, Jess. You'd look a bit green if someone had sliced you open, rummaged around with your insides and then stitched you back up again with a needle."

"Yuk." Jess screwed up her nose. She fished about in her plastic bag and pulled out a pile of dog-eared magazines. "I know people are supposed to give you cards or flowers in the hospital but I couldn't find any, so I brought you some pony magazines. I've read them already. There's a really good story in one of them about a ghost rider and a lost foal..." Jess hovered by Tom's hospital bed. She could hear herself blabbering on and on.

Tom was in a semi-private room and his bed was by the window. Opposite, a girl of about Jess's age slept soundly. There were dark circles under her eyes, but her hair was bright gold.

"That's Mary," Tom said, following Jess's eye.

"She's got a pony."

"Lucky her," Jess said as she sat down on the bed. "Nick said you wanted me to come and see you," she blurted out, curiosity getting the better of her.

Tom smiled. "So you're not here to wish me a speedy recovery?" he teased.

Jess looked downcast. "No. I mean..." she stopped and laughed. "Sorry, Tom. Of course I'm here to see how you are. But..."

"You're right," Tom interrupted her. "We've got a proposition to make to you. Me and Nick, that is. Nick said I should be the one to tell you, but he's backing this all the way. It's about Southdown," Tom explained. "I won't be able to ride, so would you like to take my place?"

There was silence. Jess knew it was her turn to speak, but she didn't know what to say. She was going to ride at Southdown!

"I'm no replacement for you Tom," she managed at last. "You're a much better rider than me."

"Well obviously no one expects you to do as well as *me*," Tom grinned. "Oh boy, I sounded just like Charlie then, didn't I?"

"Exactly," Jess agreed happily.

"But I think you'll have a good chance at placing," Tom continued seriously. "I'll be out of here by then and I'll be able to come and cheer you on."

"Oh, that would be excellent!" Jess cried.

"So how's Chancey, Jess? Is he pining away for me?" Tom asked.

"He's fine. But he does look kind of sad," Jess said, trying to drag her mind back to normal conversation as little bubbles of excitement burst in her stomach. "Don't worry," she continued. "We've all explained where you are and that you'll be back soon. He understands."

"Of course he does," Tom agreed. "He's a very intelligent horse. Oh look, here's my mom."

Jess turned around to see Tom's mother walking toward them, tall and elegant. Jess stood up to greet her. She had only met Mrs. Buchanan a few times and she didn't want to make a bad impression.

But as Mrs. Buchanan came nearer, the smile froze on Jess's face. Walking a few paces behind her, jacket bundled under his arm, was a stocky man. A man whose face Jess remembered well.

"You!" Jess croaked, as the man drew up alongside her. Ignoring Mrs. Buchanan's surprised expression, Jess spoke again. "You're the man with the runaway pony!"

65

8

EXPLANATIONS

Jess stood and stared. She knew she was being rude but she just couldn't help it. The last time she had seen this man he had been chasing a palomino pony into Sandy Lane Stables. Jess stared some more.

"What's the matter, Jess?" Tom began.

Mrs. Buchanan looked shocked at her behavior, but Jess couldn't move. She was face to face with this man – this thief! She didn't know what to do. He peered at her now and a smile spread slowly across his face.

"I recognize you!" he exclaimed at last. "You're the young lady who helped me catch Goldie the other morning!" He turned to the girl in the bed opposite Tom, who was just waking up. "Mary... this is the girl I told you about... the one who helped me with Goldie."

Mary turned and rubbed her eyes. She propped

herself up on her pillows and smiled at Jess.

"So is Goldie your pony?" Jess stammered slowly.

"Not mine," the man explained. "She's Mary's actually. You were terrific. I was kind of upset that morning. You see, Mary had been rushed into the hospital the night before and I was taking Goldie to be taken care of by some friends. I was trying to load her into the trailer, but I wasn't doing a very good job of it. That's why she spooked and bolted. If you hadn't caught her, I don't know what would have happened."

"She's a beautiful pony." Jess wanted to say more, but she was still in shock.

"She's lovely, isn't she?" Mary said eagerly, her eyes shining. "I miss her so much. What's your name?" she asked.

"Jess. Jess Adams."

"I'm Bob Hughes," said the man. "And this, as you know by now, is my daughter, Mary."

Mary smiled at Jess who still looked dazed.

"Would you like some of Tom's orange juice Jess? You're looking a little sick." Tom's mother was full of concern.

"No, I..." Jess started.

Then Tom began to laugh. "Ouch my stitches!" he yelped. "I'm sure I heard that pony was stolen," he continued when the pain had subsided.

"Stolen?" Mary's father looked astonished.

Of course, Tom didn't know that Goldie wasn't the same pony as Golddust. Jess shook her head and began to explain until at last it all came out. About mistaking Goldie for Golddust and about Belinda and – even worse – about reporting it all to the police.

Mary's dad laughed at this. "So I'm a wanted man now am I?"

But Mary was quiet. "Poor Belinda," she said. "Her pony's still missing."

Jess nodded in silent agreement. One mystery had been solved. The palomino pony Jess had caught running into the stable grounds hadn't been stolen at all. She was safe and well... unlike Golddust.

* * * * * * * * * * * * * * *

"Concentrate!" Nick called. "Come on Jess, you're letting Minstrel get away with murder. He'll run out if you don't check him."

"Sorry Nick," Jess mumbled. She shortened Minstrel's reins and turned again toward the first jump. Urging him on, she balanced the little pony so that he met the fence at exactly the right spot and they flew over the cross poles with inches to spare.

"Better," said Nick. "Much better."

It was Easter Saturday and the Southdown entrants were having a special lesson. The show was less than two weeks away now.

"We've got the early evenings," Nick had reassured them. "It's still light enough to see what's going on. Don't worry, you're all doing very well."

"Tom gets out of the hospital today," Rosie said as they rode back to the stables at the end of the lesson. "I heard Nick talking to his mom."

"I wonder how Mary is," Jess said. She had told Rosie – and Belinda – all about Mary and Goldie.

"She must miss Goldie a lot," Rosie said.

"Not as much as Belinda misses Golddust I bet," said Jess.

Both girls were quiet for a moment. They hadn't found Golddust at Ash Hill on Thursday and there weren't any more horse sales for a while. Belinda had put posters up all around the area, asking for information, but so far there had been no response. It seemed like the end of the trail for the moment. For now, the Southdown Show loomed and for Jess at least, there was no more time to search.

Feeling guilty that she couldn't help Belinda any more, Jess had asked her to come to Southdown. But Belinda had been hesitant.

"I'm not sure, Jess," she had said. "I had been hoping to ride Golddust at Southdown. I don't know if I'd feel right going there without her."

Jess replayed this conversation in her head now as she led Minstrel into the yard.

"Don't untack Minstrel, Jess," Nick said, interrupting her thoughts. "He's got a lesson in a minute."

Jess was surprised. "OK," she said. "But I thought I was booked on him for a trail ride."

"Sorry about that," Nick said. "You'll have to ride someone else. Let's see. Which horse can you ride instead?" He paused for a moment, mentally checking off the list of Sandy Lane ponies in his mind. "It'll have to be Storm Cloud," he said finally. He shook his head, but there was a grin in his voice.

"Storm Cloud?" Jess breathed. "Really?"

"Lucky you," Rosie whispered.

"She's the only one available," Nick smiled. "Anyway, it's the least I can do, seeing as I'm commandeering Minstrel for a lesson with our old friend, Petronella Slater. Well don't stand there. You better get Stormy tacked up."

"I'm going," Jess said quickly, before Nick had a chance to change his mind.

Fifteen minutes later the eleven o'clock ride was ready to leave Sandy Lane. Jess kept an eye out for Petronella, but there was no sign of her. As Sarah led the ride on Feather, Jess looked back at the stables to see Nick checking his watch and muttering angrily. It looked as if Petronella was late.

"Walk on everybody," Sarah called and Jess drew her attention back to the ride. Sarah turned Feather to the gate and the ride clattered out of the stable grounds and down the lane.

For the next hour, Jess planned to forget about Petronella; forget about mistaking Bob Hughes for a thief; forget about Golddust even. Something told her that the chances of finding the pony were getting slimmer and slimmer every day. She tried to ignore the guilty feeling that she was letting Belinda down, but she had important things of her own to think about. Anyway, right now, she wanted to concentrate utterly and completely on Storm Cloud. It was such a treat to be riding her.

The little gray's step was light and easy. Her ears pricked forward, alert and attentive. They had reached the open fields at the back of the stables and Sarah gathered the ride around her.

"Those who want to can gallop to the end of the field. There are three cross-country fences to jump. Can you see them?"

Jess looked ahead and saw three low tree trunks lying in a row.

At Sarah's signal the ride began to gallop. Storm Cloud was first and she didn't need any more encouragement. Jess gathered up her reins and nudged her forward, moving smoothly from a trot to a canter and then into a gallop. Three long strides and a signal from Jess, and Storm Cloud had cleared the first tree trunk, then the second and the third.

On Stormy's back, Jess felt the smoothness of movement and hardly even noticed as they sailed through the air. She brought Storm Cloud to a neat and collected stop at the end of the field. Rosie drew Pepper to a halt beside her, her cheeks were flushed and eyes were glowing. Pepper snorted heartily.

"You looked fantastic!" Rosie cried. "Storm Cloud

jumps like a deer."

"She's just fantastic, isn't she?" Jess sighed happily.

9

SOUTHDOWN AT LAST!

The next few days flew by... before Jess knew it, there was only a week to go, and then four days. Then it was the day after tomorrow and now – now it was Friday evening and tomorrow was the Southdown Show!

Jess wandered restlessly around the house, unable to concentrate on anything or settle anywhere. She picked up the TV remote control and flicked from channel to channel but there was nothing she wanted to watch that evening.

Jess padded into the kitchen and opened the refrigerator door, contemplating the choice inside.

"Close the door, Jess," said her dad. "You're letting all the cold air out."

"What you need is a warm bath and an early night,"

her mother sympathized. "Stop worrying, Jess."

"I'm not worried," Jess said crossly. "Just excited."

Her mother smiled at her. Jess had been afraid her parents wouldn't approve of her riding in a horse show because it meant more time spent with ponies and not on her schoolwork. But they had been surprisingly encouraging.

"We'll all be there to watch. We wouldn't miss it for the world," they had said.

Jess went to bed early that night. She didn't think she'd sleep at all. She put her head on the pillow and tried to fill her mind with pleasant thoughts of jumping ponies. The next thing she knew, daylight was streaming in through the curtains and it was seven in the morning. Saturday and Southdown!

"We'll be by the ringside if we don't see you first," her mother said at breakfast. "Now, are you *sure* you don't want a lift to Sandy Lane?"

But Jess wanted to ride her bicycle as she always did.

"It's probably some sort of crazy good luck routine, Mom. I'd let her do it," her brother, Jack, muttered as they waved her off.

Sandy Lane was a buzz of activity as Jess rode into the yard with the plastic bag containing her show gear hooked over the handlebars.

The horse vans stood ready for loading with their precious cargo. Riders were scurrying around grooming, braiding manes, picking out hooves. Jess was about to fling her bicycle down. Then she had second thoughts and leaned it carefully against the wall of the tack room. Alex and Kate called out to her. "We're your cheerleading team today – good luck Jess!"

Charlie was in Napoleon's stall, vigorously brushing the horse's brown coat. "A perfect job," he said, standing back to admire his work.

"You've missed a little," Jess grinned, leaving Charlie inspecting every inch of Napoleon's coat for imaginary specks of dirt.

She walked over to Minstrel, who stood waiting patiently, peering over the stall door. The pony snickered gently when he saw Jess, and his nostrils quivered with quiet excitement.

"You know you're going to a show, boy, don't you?" Jess whispered in his ear. "Well, it's not just any show you see. It's the Southdown show, and I know you're going to be awesome."

"CLANG!"

Pepper's stall door swung open and Jess's peaceful moment was interrupted by a clatter of hooves and a flurry of flying feet as the little pony jogged out of his stall, into the yard and off down the lane. Rosie followed close behind.

"He's spooking like crazy," Rosie called breathlessly over her shoulder.

She bolted after the little pony, but Pepper saw her coming and, with one effortless leap, he had cleared the pond and landed in the grass on the other side. Unconcerned, he trotted lightly toward the overhanging trees and, straining his neck, he began to munch at the leaves. Twigs caught in his mane, making a complete mess of the tidy braids Rosie had spent hours on.

"Too bad Rosie," Charlie called as Rosie hurried off to catch him.

When each of the ponies was almost ready, Nick called the team together.

"Van loading," he said. "You must all be responsible for getting your pony into the van as calmly and as swiftly as possible. So here's the order. Minstrel first, then Pepper in this one. Sarah will drive it. I'll be driving the other one with Napoleon, Feather and Storm Cloud in it."

"Storm Cloud?" Jess was immediately alert. "But, I didn't know she was coming. And Feather too? Who'll be riding them, Nick?"

"Not so fast, Jess," Nick smiled. "Storm Cloud and Feather won't be entering any competitions today. But they will be competing soon and they need to get used to a show atmosphere."

Jess squirmed with embarrassment at her eager outburst.

"Everything ready?" Nick was saying now. "Let's go!"

"Wait for me!" A breathless voice made them all look around. Belinda, dressed in pale beige britches and a dark jacket, climbed out of her mother's car and ran toward them.

"You came after all!" Jess cried. Belinda stood in the grass and smiled at Jess.

"Well, there didn't seem much point moping around at home," Belinda explained. "The least I can do is come and help cheer you guys on."

"Let's hope you've brought a few miracles with you then," Jess grinned ruefully. "I'll need them if I'm going to jump anything today."

And then they were off at last – to Southdown and the show.

As the Sandy Lane horse vans pulled into the Southdown showground, Jess felt a swirling mix of excitement and fear race through her. Everywhere was bustling with activity. Official stewards with clipboards ran around, barking out instructions and organizing everyone. Vans and trailers of all shapes and sizes were everywhere they looked. Tied to each trailer were horses and ponies in various states of grooming. A perfectly poised little girl on a tiny roan mare popped backward and forward over a practice jump with effortless ease. Riders in tailored black jackets and cream britches strode past confidently, greeting each other.

Over in the main field there were stalls and marquees selling everything from saddle soap to riding hats, hot dogs to smoked salmon. Was it really only last year that she and Rosie had been enthralled spectators here, the chances of them taking part only a dream? And now they were official competitors!

They tethered the ponies and gave them a final grooming while Nick went off to check everyone in.

"I'll meet you by the ring," he called as he left, "and we'll walk around the course together."

Jess struggled into her show jacket. She turned to Rosie excitedly.

"Can you believe we're really here, Rosie?" she breathed.

"I would be excited if I wasn't feeling so nervous," Rosie groaned in reply.

Jess looked around for Tom. He had promised he would be here. She hadn't seen him since the day at the hospital. She hoped he would be well enough to come.

They met up with Nick again at the show ring. He handed out their numbers and then led them around the course. Belinda came too, for moral support, and Alex and Kate followed on behind. The course was difficult and the fences looked big. Jess didn't like the look of the combination, but Nick had some words of advice.

"Keep the impulsion as you come around the corner and don't over ride it, Jess," he warned her before he left for the competitors' tent.

"Have you jumped a course as hard as this, Belinda?" Jess asked.

"Um, no, actually," Belinda grinned ruefully. "It looks pretty challenging. You'll just have to take it steady and, well, enjoy it."

"Easier said than done," Jess groaned, but her

insides had calmed down a little. She was even almost looking forward to jumping. It was time to go and warm Minstrel up.

"I'll meet you back at the van," Belinda said. "I'm going to have a look at the dressage."

"And I promised to meet my mom by the stewards' tent," Rosie called as Belinda went. "I won't be long."

Jess waved goodbye and followed Alex and Kate back to the Sandy Lane horse vans.

"Is Nick with you?" Sarah asked as they approached.

"No, he had to check something out at the competitors' tent," Alex answered.

"I'd better go and find him," said Sarah. "There's some man... says he knows Nick, who's eager to buy Storm Cloud. I said she wasn't for sale but he's very insistent. He's just gone off to find his wife. I need Nick to straighten this one out. Will you keep an eye on the horses? Watch out for Pepper. He's been spooking a little."

Buy Storm Cloud? Jess shook her head. Surely they would never sell her, but if this man was a friend of Nick's...

She went over to the gray mare who stood grazing in the shade, ears alert to the sounds around her, her tail twitching nervously. As Jess approached, Storm Cloud lifted her head and snickered. She nuzzled her soft nose into Jess's shoulder and her tail relaxed.

"Don't worry, Stormy," Jess whispered. "Nick and Sarah would never sell you. You're far too precious to them. And to me," she added silently.

Suddenly, a small brown dog tore around the corner of the van yapping and snapping. Storm Cloud started but Jess laid a steadying hand on her neck and she was still again.

"Rags! Come back here," a child cried.

But Rags took no notice as he darted and weaved between the ponies' hooves.

Pepper shifted nervously and, at the small dog's shrill barking, he kicked out in a blind panic, hitting Minstrel squarely and sharply on the fetlock. Minstrel whinnied in pain and reared up. When he landed again, he was limping ominously.

Jess held onto Storm Cloud while Alex and Kate did their best to calm Minstrel and Pepper. Rags scampered off and his small owner finally caught up with him. But the damage had been done. Minstrel was limping badly. Nick and Sarah came running up but Jess knew from their faces that they had seen everything. It didn't look good.

"Oh no," Nick groaned as he ran a reassuring and calming hand down Minstrel's foreleg. "I think we'd better get the vet to come and look at this. It doesn't look like you'll be riding Minstrel today, I'm afraid."

As Nick made his way to the secretary's tent, Jess stared in disbelief. This couldn't be happening. Poor Minstrel. Poor her! Was this the end of her Southdown dream?

Jess didn't have time to dwell on it though, for in an instant, her thoughts were disturbed as Belinda came charging up the field.

"Listen, oh listen everyone."

"Slow down," Sarah said as Belinda gulped for breath. "Now, what's the matter?"

"I've seen her. She's here," Belinda gasped.

"Who's here?" Sarah asked.

"Golddust," Belinda cried. "She's here at Southdown!"

10

STRIKING GOLD

Golddust! In all the excitement preparing for Southdown, Jess had completely forgotten about her. Belinda's words were greeted with stunned silence. It was all too much to take in. Finally, it was Sarah who spoke.

"Are you sure, Belinda?" she asked.

"Of course I am," Belinda cried. "I'd recognize Golddust anywhere." She stopped short as she sensed the subdued atmosphere, the glum faces. "What's happened here?" she finished.

Jess found her voice and quickly explained about the runaway dog and Minstrel's accident, but before she had a chance to say more, Sarah had taken charge of the situation.

"I need to stay and wait for Nick, Jess," she said.

"Can you go with Belinda and find out what's going on? But be very careful what you do and what you say. Come and get us if there are any problems." And when she saw Jess hesitating, she said urgently, "Go on now – and hurry!"

Jess nodded and the two girls darted off through the crowd. The hustle and bustle around them only added to the confusion in Jess's head.

"She was over here," said Belinda as she led the way through the throng to a small copse of trees. At first Jess couldn't make out where Belinda was pointing. She screwed up her eyes to get a better glimpse of the ponies. Blacks, bays, a roan and a gray. And suddenly she saw her. Standing slightly apart from the others, kicking her heels and dancing on the spot was a beautiful palomino pony with mane and tail the color of white gold. On her forehead was a small circle of white hair.

"Golddust!" Belinda breathed.

"Wait a minute, Belinda," Jess said, grabbing her arm. "There's someone with her. Look!"

A small girl with long braided hair was hanging desperately onto the end of Golddust's lead rope with both hands, trying in vain to calm the jumpy pony. But with every tug of the rope and with every yank of her hands, Golddust became even more frantic. Belinda winced.

"I can't stand it, Jess," she cried. "That girl is scaring Golddust half to death. I have to go." She raced toward them.

"Wait for me!" Jess called, and ran after her.

Belinda slowed down as she neared Golddust, and began to talk in low soothing tones. "It's all right girl, here I am," she said.

At the sound of her voice, Golddust's ears twitched forward.

As Belinda drew up alongside her and laid a soothing hand across her pony's neck, Golddust whinnied again, and this time the sound wasn't of fear, but one of sheer pleasure. Belinda buried her head in Golddust's mane.

"It's all right my beauty," Jess could hear her saying, "I'm here. I've found you at last!"

The girl hanging onto Golddust looked relieved.

"Thank you, oh thank you for calming her down!" she cried. "I don't know what I would have done if you hadn't come along."

Jess looked at the small upturned face streaked with sweat and tears and felt sorry for her. She looked very young and bewildered.

"Are your parents here?" she asked.

"They were, but they've gone to look at a pony they want to buy for my sister."

"Is this your pony, then?" Jess asked, pointing to Golddust.

"No, she's my sister's. I'm not into riding. We haven't had her long and she's sort of a handful. Daddy's gone to look at another pony that might be more manageable. Oh–" she stopped abruptly. "I'm not supposed to talk to strangers. Who are you?"

Jess smiled. "I'm Jess," she said. "And this is Belinda."

"My name's Sally," the girl replied. "My sister's supposed to be riding in the junior jumping today. Rather her than me – this pony's practically wild."

"She isn't wild, she's just frightened," Belinda said lifting her head and tuning into Sally's stream of chatter. "Wait a minute – where did you get this pony?"

"Daddy bought her," Sally replied. "Why?"

"Sally," Jess said as softly as she could. "This pony is called Golddust. She belongs to Belinda. She was stolen from her a few weeks ago."

"Stolen! But that's impossible." Sally's eyes widened in disbelief. "Daddy paid for her... he did."

"I'm sure he did," Belinda said quickly. "But she had already been stolen from me."

"Oh." Sally fell into a stunned silence.

Jess shifted uncomfortably. This was the last thing she had expected... to find Golddust in the hands of someone else.

"I think we ought to find your parents," Jess said quickly. However nice Sally was, the fact remained that her dad had bought a stolen pony, and would have to give it back.

"Oh good." A look of relief spread across Sally's face. "Here they are now. And my sister's with them too."

Jess turned to follow Sally's eager gaze. Sure enough, a girl was striding purposefully toward them, closely followed by two grownups. The girl was dressed in an immaculate black riding jacket, cream britches and shiny black boots. She was horribly familiar.

"Petronella Slater!" Jess cried.

"You!" Petronella sneered.

Behind her, talking in loud voices, strode Mr. Slater and a woman with the same disdainful expression as Petronella, so that Jess could only imagine she was her mother.

"What a shame Nick Brooks wouldn't sell that lovely gray pony. And after you rode her so well at Sandy Lane, Pet," the woman trilled.

"I didn't *want* that pony anyway," Petronella hissed.

Jess couldn't believe her ears. They must be talking about Storm Cloud. But Petronella *hadn't* ridden her well. She had been arrogant and reckless and had frightened poor Stormy half to death. What nerve – if only Petronella's mother knew the truth. Jess's thoughts were interrupted by Sally's anxious voice.

"Dad, come quick. Petronella's pony's been stolen!" she cried.

"What are you talking about, Sal?" Petronella said quickly. "She's right here. Look."

"No," Sally cried. "I mean she's a stolen pony!"

"What garbage," Mr. Slater boomed. "Of course she's not stolen. I bought her fair and square."

"Look, I'm sure you did," Belinda burst out. "But she is my pony and I can prove it. She's freezemarked right here." She pointed to a number on the little

86

palomino's neck. "And I have all the documents at home."

Mrs. Slater looked furious. "I knew there was something fishy about that man who sold her to you," she barked. "I told you so at the time, Colin. But you didn't listen to me. You never do."

Mr. Slater looked harassed. "Oh dear," he groaned. "But Pet wanted that pony so badly. How was I to know..." He paused anxiously. "Look," he said at last. "I think we should call the police, resolve this right away."

Jess couldn't agree more. Right now, her head was beginning to ache with trying to think sensibly.

"Why don't we go and get Nick," she said to Belinda.

"No!" Petronella spat.

Mr. Slater looked straight at Jess for the first time. "Don't I know you?" he asked.

"Yes," Jess had to admit. "I took Petronella out for a ride at Sandy Lane. She rode Storm Cloud," she said. *Or tried to*, she couldn't help adding in her head.

"Ah yes," Mr. Slater smiled affably. "It was after that we got Petronella her own pony. She had such a good time that day. And she told me how well she had ridden."

Jess shot Petronella a quick glance. Petronella shifted uncomfortably. She cast her eyes downward and kicked at the grass with her heel. For a brief moment Jess considered telling Mr. Slater the truth about that day, but what was the point? Petronella obviously had him wrapped around her little finger. Besides, the fact remained, there were more important things to sort out. Mr. Slater seemed to have read her mind.

"Look, I'm going to get the police," he said. "I want to straighten this out once and for all."

"Yes, I think you'd better, Colin," Mrs. Slater barked. "What would people say if they found out we'd been handling stolen goods?"

Jess was relieved that things were starting to get moving. Which was just as well, because a terrible thought had just struck her. Minstrel! Jess looked at her watch. Time was running out. The junior jumping would be starting soon. Was Minstrel fit enough to enter? Jess had to find out what was going on.

"I have to get back," she cried to the startled Slaters. "It's Minstrel," she explained to Belinda.

"Of course." Belinda understood immediately. "Go on, Jess. Everything is under control here."

And so Jess raced back to her Sandy Lane teammates. When she arrived at the horse vans, she was greeted by a sea of glum faces. Rosie was the first to speak. Jess could tell that she was dying to know about Golddust, but news of Minstrel came first.

"It doesn't look good, Jess," Rosie said. "The vet left a while ago, and Nick and Sarah have been in a conspiratorial huddle forever. We're just waiting to find out what's going on."

Jess groaned. Time was running out. They would be starting the junior jumping any minute. Charlie was mounted and raring to go and Rosie was circling Pepper, warming the piebald pony up. They were low numbers, twelve and fourteen respectively, so they had to get a move on. Jess was number thirty-eight – second last. She sighed. There didn't seem much point in wearing it any more. Minstrel stood patiently under a tree, ominously favoring his right foreleg. Jess walked over and began to stroke him gently.

At long last, Nick and Sarah stopped talking and came over.

"It's bad news, I'm afraid, Jess," Nick said. "Minstrel's got a badly bruised left foreleg. He'll be all right, but there's no way he can jump today."

Jess lowered her head and tried to fight back the tears that welled in her eyes. She had expected this but it was still a bitter disappointment. To be given the chance to ride at Southdown and then to have it so cruelly snatched away from her at the last moment was almost more than she could handle.

But now Sarah was speaking and although Jess tried to focus on the words, it was a while before she understood. At last Sarah got through to her.

"Did you hear that Jess?" she said. "You can ride after all."

"Ride after all, but how?" Jess was confused.

"It's Sarah's idea," Nick explained. "But I agree with her. We're going to let you ride Storm Cloud, Jess – if you want to, that is. She's an excellent jumper and you've ridden her well before. I'm not saying it will be easy, but if you take it steady I'm sure you'll be all right. So what do you say?"

What could she say? Jess could only beam. She saw Rosie beaming back at her.

To ride Storm Cloud would be a dream come true. She felt proud that Nick and Sarah had so much faith in her. Minstrel was injured and that was terrible, but she had been given another chance. She had to make the most of it.

"Oh thank you so much. Thanks Nick, thank you Sarah," Jess gasped. "I will ride Storm Cloud. We'll do our best to make Sandy Lane proud of us!"

11

SHOWJUMPING

Storm Cloud stood steady and alert as Jess sprang lightly onto her back. She followed Rosie and Charlie to the warm-up ring to warm up. As they drew near, Alex and Kate spotted them and came over. Wide-eyed, they immediately wanted to know what had happened to Minstrel, and why Jess was riding Storm Cloud. Jess hurriedly explained.

"Poor Minstrel. But how exciting for you," Kate exclaimed. "We've been watching the jumping so far. Some of the fences are really difficult."

"They're not too bad," Alex said calmly. "Jump five, the square parallel, seems to be causing problems. And judging the combination at the sixth fence looks tricky too."

"Jess, Jess!" an eager voice at stirrup level called

and Jess looked down to see her little sister Em gazing up at her.

"What a beautiful pony," said Em.

Her mom and dad joined her. "You look very professional Jess. Good luck," they smiled.

Jess smiled happily when suddenly an announcement over the loudspeakers caught her ear.

"Competitor number ten, Belinda Lang on Golddust. This is a rider change."

What? Jess could hardly believe it. Belinda must have straightened everything out with the Slaters. Jess jumped down from Storm Cloud and tethered him at the van. Then she made her way to watch as Belinda and Golddust entered the ring. She felt as nervous as if it were already her turn.

Golddust tossed her head playfully, her flaxen mane blowing freely in the breeze. She held her magnificent tail up high and the sun glinted and danced on her golden coat. Belinda sat poised and calm, controlling Golddust with no perceptible movement, seemingly unaware of all around her. But then she caught Jess's eye and grinned uncontrollably. Jess saw her confidence and began to relax. She would enjoy watching Belinda. She knew they were in for a treat.

With the ring of the bell, Golddust cantered off and took the first fence with easy strides. She hardly seemed to notice there were jumps beneath her feet as she all but flew over the bars and onto the brush, then the gate. Then she was over the difficult square parallel and onto the combination. One and two and it was cleared before Jess had time to blink. Now they were at the triple bar, almost as tall as Golddust herself, but Belinda urged the pony on and they landed lightly, and onto the final wall. Jumping clear, they were finished and out of the ring. A roar from the crowd signaled their appreciation and Jess exhaled slowly as Rosie gasped in delight beside her.

"Clear round," boomed the announcer.

"Wow, they were awesome!" said Rosie.

"She's good!" Alex said. "Really, really good."

"That'll take some beating," said Kate, shaking her head.

"Well, I'm going to give it a try," Charlie grinned, bringing them all back down to earth with a bump. Wish me luck!"

"Good luck, Charlie!" everyone called as the loudspeakers announced that competitor number eleven had clocked up four faults.

But Jess said nothing. She was thinking about the way Belinda and Golddust had looked together; about the practiced ease with which Belinda handled Golddust; the way in which the pony seemed to have complete trust and faith in Belinda, and responded eagerly to her every command. As Belinda came up to them, leading Golddust, Jess joined in with the congratulations of the others. She wanted to ask about Petronella, but now wasn't the time. Belinda was flushed with pleasure.

"It's all thanks to Sandy Lane," she said. "I would never have come to Southdown today if it hadn't been for you. And now I've found Golddust and I don't care if I win or lose. I think right at this moment I'm the happiest person alive."

"Competitor number twelve. Charlie Marshall on Napoleon," came the announcement.

"Quick, we shouldn't miss this," Kate said eagerly.

Charlie certainly cut an imposing figure as he rode Napoleon confidently into the ring.

"He's gorgeous," whispered a girl in front.

"Yeah, and the rider's not bad either," her friend replied.

Kate and Jess nudged each other in fits of giggles. But they were soon lost in the swiftness and capability of Charlie's ride. Before they knew it, he had ridden triumphantly out of the ring.

"Clear round!" the announcer called.

"Oh no, it's me now," Rosie cried as competitor number thirteen sent the square parallel crashing to the ground. "Wish me luck," she called, riding away.

"Go on Rosie," Jess whispered fiercely.

Slowly and steadily and with great determination, Rosie and Pepper cleared the ascending oxer and the bars. They clipped the top of the brush but the jump remained intact. Next it was the parallel, the combination, and finally the wall. They were over and clear. It wasn't fast, but it was effective. Pepper stalked out of the ring, tail held high.

"Way to go! That was amazing Rosie," Jess cried as the pair came toward her.

"I was a little slow." Rosie wrinkled her nose.

"But you jumped steadily and clear," Jess reassured her.

Nick joined their little group. "Well, I have to say that things are looking very good so far. Two clear rounds for Sandy Lane. And a clear for Belinda, our honorary member."

Belinda's eyes shone with delight at Nick's words. Jess smiled wanly. Would their good luck last? It was all up to her. Quietly she took herself away from the crowd and began to warm Storm Cloud up. Round and round they walked in the practice field, every lap bringing them closer to their turn. In the show ring, the competition continued until at last competitor thirty-seven left the ring, a trail of spectacular destruction in her wake.

"Sixteen faults for Amanda Matthews on Cinnamon," the announcer confirmed.

"It's going to be a tough one, Storm Cloud," Jess murmured into the pony's alert ears.

"You'll be fine, Jess." A voice at her side startled her. She looked down to see...

"Tom! Oh you made it. Great! How are you feeling?"

"Weak," Tom smiled. "But excited too. I'm looking forward to seeing you jump. There have been eight clear rounds so far – yours will be the ninth." Jess's heart soared and suddenly she didn't feel so bad. If Tom thought she could do it, well... she'd try her very best.

"Thanks Tom," she grinned. Then she leaned over to whisper in Storm Cloud's ear. "It's our turn now, girl. Let's show them what we can do."

Circling Storm Cloud as she waited for their number to be called, Jess tried to shut everything else out – the hum of the crowd, the activity around her. Suddenly a voice echoed across the field.

"Competitor number thirty-eight, Jess Adams on Storm Cloud."

They trotted into the ring. Suddenly Jess was nervous again. This was it. She was here. She was really going to jump at Southdown! She felt Storm Cloud quiver with anticipation and bent down to pat her dappled neck.

"We can do it together, Storm Cloud. I know we can!" she whispered.

She trotted Storm Cloud around the edge of the ring, battling hard to keep her nerves from interfering with her concentration. Suddenly the bell sounded.

"Let's take our time, Stormy," Jess murmured. "The clock isn't ticking yet."

And before she knew it, the first fence was behind them. Jess felt a surge of confidence. The competition had begun! Now they were clear on course for the bars.

"Jump," she breathed as she urged Storm Cloud forward. Don't look down, she reminded herself, and kept her gaze firmly fixed between Storm Cloud's alert ears. The spirited pony knew exactly what was expected of her and gathering her strength she soared through the air, leaving inches of space between her and the jump.

Onward they rode, up and over the brush and toward the gate. Storm Cloud reached high for the obstacle and cleared it, but she overbalanced on landing and Jess was flung forward. Swiftly she tried to right herself as she turned Storm Cloud in the approach to the parallel. But Jess felt she was still leaning too far forward. She was losing contact. Storm Cloud sensed Jess's dilemma and knew what was expected of her. Valiantly she attempted the jump. As the pony's head came up, Jess was struck on the chin. She bit her lip heavily and tasted blood. Her pain increased as she heard Storm Cloud's hind legs rap the top pole. Jess's heart stopped and time stood still. Then she regained her balance and cantered on, all the time straining to hear the thud of pole hitting grass. She couldn't look back, but the gasp of relief from the crowd told her it was all right. The pole had stayed in place and Jess had been offered a chance to prove herself.

"Way to go, Storm Cloud," she breathed. "I won't make that mistake again. We can do it!"

With renewed confidence, she rode Storm Cloud straight and square toward the combination. Storm Cloud flicked her tail and thundered on. But Jess was prepared.

"Steady, steady," Jess chanted under her breath.

One, two, three, jump! And they were over the first combination. Storm Cloud flew through the air. Touchdown! Take off! And they were soaring again.

Clear and away. They flew over the cross poles as the final fence loomed. They jumped the wall with ease and then they were finished and out of the ring. Jess barely had time to catch her breath before she realized what had happened.

"Oh good job, Storm Cloud," she cried, flinging her arms forward around the pony's neck. "We did it!"

As if to confirm this fact, the announcer boomed out the result.

"Clear round for competitor number thirty-eight, Jess Adams on Storm Cloud."

Everyone gathered around to congratulate her.

"Amazing, Jess," Nick approached her and gave Storm Cloud a pat. "You rode very well."

Jess glowed with happiness and pride. But it wasn't over yet. She was through to the jump-off – against the clock this time – and she needed to gather her thoughts and regain her composure.

She led Storm Cloud off to cool down beneath the trees before their big moment arrived. She knew her friends would be jumping too, but all she could think about now was how to get the best performance out of Storm Cloud – how to ride like the wind.

There were ten riders in all for the final competition. Jess was jumping fifth, Belinda was ninth. Charlie was seventh. Poor Rosie was to jump first. As much as Jess wanted to cheer Rosie on, this time the suspense was too much for her, and she knew she couldn't watch.

When her number was finally called, she had no

idea what time she had to beat. She would just have to jump the round of her life, Storm Cloud seemed to have picked up on the urgency of it all and skipped and danced beneath her.

"This is it, girl," Jess whispered.

"Good luck, Jess," Tom called from the side of the field.

Storm Cloud tossed her smoke-gray mane in nonchalant reply and trotted once again into the ring. Jess held her in check with just the lightest touch of the reins.

"Relax, relax," she whispered softly as she circled Storm Cloud. And then there was the ring of the bell and they were off! Swift and steady to the first jump. A light tap of her heels and Storm Cloud was over and riding squarely for the bars. Up and away and they were down again and Jess felt as light as a feather. Turning nimbly, she headed Storm Cloud for the brush, counting the strides with every thunder of Storm Cloud's hooves. One and two and three and they were over and then they had cleared the gate before Jess had time to catch her breath.

Now they were entering the turn for the parallel. But this time, Jess was ready for it. She was in control. She checked Storm Cloud and set her square and then they were racing toward the jump. Jess felt Storm Cloud's front legs tuck well underneath her as she sprung high into the air and over the pole. Clear!

Now was the combination and it was one, two and over. Storm Cloud turned on a dime as she rounded the corner. They flew over the triple bar and now there was just the wall to go. Storm Cloud took that in her stride and they were clear! Jess's heart pounded and reverberated loudly in her ears as she clasped her arms around Storm Cloud's neck.

"Fantastic!" she cried.

"Jess Adams, clear in fifty-three seconds," the announcer boomed.

Jess was exhilarated. It sounded fast, but was it fast enough?

"Great job Jess!" Nick called. "You really got the best out of Storm Cloud!"

"Oh Jess, that was amazing!" Rosie cried as she rushed up. "You did much better than me. Pepper clipped the wall with his heels. That's four faults automatically."

Alex grinned broadly at her. "That was some performance Jess. I think you have a shot at a ribbon. Way to go."

Jess shook her head. "It was all Storm Cloud," she protested.

They all turned in time to see the next competitor crash into the brush and net herself four faults.

And then it was Charlie's turn. As he rode into the ring once more, Jess had to admit they looked magnificent. Napoleon's healthy, brown coat shone in the bright sunlight and Charlie pressed him on over the jumps. He seemed to have remembered all Nick's words of advice, for this time he didn't rush the course but took it steadily and swiftly. And then he had finished and was clear.

"Charlie Marshall on Napoleon, jumping clear in forty-nine seconds!" echoed the announcer.

"He was fantastic!" Jess cried.

"He's in the lead!" Rosie shouted at Jess's side.

The next rider, a tiny girl on top of a sprightly little roan pony jumped clear also, and the announcer confirmed this. "Melissa James, jumping clear in fifty-one seconds."

"Not as fast as Charlie," Alex muttered.

"But faster than me," Jess couldn't help thinking. Yet somehow she didn't care. She had jumped and she had jumped well. She had done her best and she was happy. Now it was time to watch Belinda.

Jess stood close to Storm Cloud as she watched Belinda enter the ring with Golddust. She gazed in silent admiration as Belinda cantered the golden pony easily around the ring.

"Wow, what a fantastic pony," a girl whispered next to Jess.

Jess stood enthralled at Belinda's performance. Swiftly and efficiently Golddust cleared the jumps in quick succession, and at what a pace!

"Clear in forty six seconds!" the announcement came. "Belinda Lang takes the lead on Golddust!"

Tears shone in Belinda's eyes as she left the ring. After all this time without her beloved pony, Belinda and Golddust had been reunited and had returned in triumph. Jess knew she and Storm Cloud had jumped superbly but it was Belinda who had been the best and really deserved to win. She was so wrapped up in her thoughts that it took Jess a few moments to take in what Rosie was saying to her.

"Come on, it's all over!" Rosie cried as the final competitor left the ring. "Belinda's won!"

"I know she has," Jess said.

"And we've got to follow her into the ring to collect our prizes," Rosie urged.

"Prizes? What for?" Jess was confused.

"You came in fourth, silly," Rosie laughed. "And I was sixth. Guess what Jess? We're winners at Southdown!"

Jess was astounded. She could hardly believe it. She climbed into Storm Cloud's saddle once more and rode into the ring.

"Get behind me Jess," Charlie grinned as he rode past. "I came second you know!"

At the side of the ring Jess saw her family, grinning with pride. Tom was there too, and Alex and Kate jumped up and down, cheering and clapping. Jess's heart jumped as she caught a glimpse of Petronella and Sally watching them closely. In the background, Nick and Sarah were talking urgently to Mr. Slater and a policeman. But nothing else mattered to Jess now. As she followed Charlie into the ring for the celebratory lap of honor she could only beam and beam.

12

RUNAWAY RETURNS

"I can't believe Mr. Slater gave Golddust back so easily in the end," said Rosie.

Jess and Rosie were sitting in the tack room at Sandy Lane on the Saturday after the Southdown Show. A can of saddle soap stood open on the table in front of them and, as they talked, they polished their way methodically through a jumbled pile of stirrup leathers.

"Well, there wasn't a lot he could do about it," said Jess. "The police told him because Golddust was stolen, she still belonged to the original owner. Petronella was furious about Belinda riding her, but her mother said she wasn't allowed to have anything more to do with a stolen pony. And it seems that what Petronella's mother says goes..."

So far the police hadn't managed to track down the

man who sold Golddust to the Slaters, although they hadn't given up hope of catching him. Golddust was back with Belinda again, and Nick and Sarah had offered Belinda the use of the spare stall at Sandy Lane on a temporary basis. With a thief still around, Belinda couldn't be careful enough.

"Who am I booked on for the 11 o'clock trail ride?" Alex strode in to join Rosie and Jess in the tack room.

"Hello Alex. You're on Hector I think," Jess said.

"What, that lumbering old thing?" Alex groaned, but he was only joking. Alex loved Hector and Jess and Rosie knew it.

"Who's a lumbering old thing?" a familiar voice inquired.

"Tom!" Jess and Rosie exclaimed together. "You're back! Are you riding today? Are you feeling better? Have you missed Chancey?"

Tom stumbled back in mock horror, fending off the barrage of questions with fake blows. "Good grief, what an onslaught," he grinned. "Well, to answer your questions. No, I'm not riding today – I'm not quite up to that yet, although I am feeling better. And – yes – yes, I have missed Chancey."

"Hey, everyone," Charlie chimed in. "Who am I riding?"

But no one had time to answer him as an angry Kate appeared at the doorway, hands on hips.

"OK, Alex, that's it!" she said, her eyes glinting furiously. "Just because your bike has a flat, it doesn't give you the right to take mine!"

"Sorry, Kate." Alex shrank guiltily into a corner. "But you took so long getting ready this morning, and your bike was just sitting there looking all shiny and tempting and..."

"Hello everybody," Belinda appeared. "I've come to take Golddust out. How's Minstrel today, Jess?"

"He's much better," Jess replied. "I'm riding him later."

Amidst the chatting and laughing Nick popped his head around the tack room door. "There's someone asking for you outside, Jess," he said.

"It's Petronella Slater. She wants a private lesson!" said Charlie. By now everyone at Sandy Lane knew Petronella's story. Jess glared at him and walked out. It was bright outside after the dimness of the tack room but when Jess could see clearly, she found herself face to face with a stocky man. It was Bob Hughes.

"I brought Goldie and Mary to see you," he smiled.

Jess blinked. Sure enough, in front of her sat Mary on top of a beautiful palomino pony.

"Goldie!" Jess breathed. "Hello Mary. Can I stroke her?"

"Of course," Mary smiled down at Jess. "It's my first ride on Goldie since I got out of the hospital," she explained. "We only live up on Ash Hill road so we thought we'd drop in and say hello."

"I'm glad you came," Jess said. "That's Belinda's pony, Golddust, over there," she said, pointing to where Golddust stood in her stall. "She's the one I confused Goldie with. They don't actually look the same at all,

105

do they?"

"No," Mary smiled. "They're completely different. Both lovely, but different."

At that moment, Belinda came out of the tack room. "Is that the runaway palomino pony?" she asked.

"Yes," said Jess. "Funny to see both Goldie and Golddust together."

"Mary!" Tom's voice called from the tack room and they all looked around. "How are you feeling?"

"Hello Tom," Mary replied as she slipped down from the saddle. "OK, I guess. You look much better."

"Thanks, I feel it."

"What a lovely pony!" Rosie, Charlie, Alex and Kate crowded eagerly around Mary. Goldie jumped back in startled surprise at all this attention and moved nearer to Golddust. The two ponies neighed gently at each other and stood nose to nose, breathing softly.

Jess stood back a little way from her friends and watched them all, eagerly chatting and laughing. She wanted to stand on the edge for a while and see what Sandy Lane looked like to an outside eye.

"It looks just great," she said to herself.

From the stall behind her came a soft whinny. Storm Cloud was hanging her head over her door as usual, her delicate gray face turned toward Jess. Jess walked slowly toward her and breathed softly into the little pony's nose.

"I haven't forgotten you, Stormy," she whispered into the pony's ear. "We'll ride again together soon. Nick promised me that."

"Come on Jess," a voice at her elbow interrupted. Rosie stood there smiling. "It's nearly 11 o'clock. Minstrel and Pepper are waiting. Let's go and tack up."

A Horse for the Summer by Michelle Bates

The first title in the Sandy Lane Stables series

There was a frantic whinny and the sound of drumming hooves reverberated around the yard as Chancey pranced down the ramp. He was certainly on his toes, but he didn't look like the sleek, well turned-out horse that Tom remembered seeing last season. He was still unclipped and his shabby winter coat was flecked with foam as feverishly he pawed the ground. No one knew what to say...

When Tom is left a prize-winning show jumper for the summer, things don't turn out quite as he hoped. Chancey is wild and unpredictable and Tom is forced to start training him in secret. But the days of summer are numbered and Chancey isn't Tom's to keep forever. At some point, he will have to give him back...

Strangers at the Stables by Michelle Bates

The third title in the Sandy Lane Stables series

> ...Thoughts jostled around in Rosie's mind as she crossed the yard. She couldn't believe how many things had gone wrong in the couple of weeks Nick and Sarah had been gone. She needed time to think. There was something worrying her, right at the back of her mind... something that held the key to it all. But what was it?

When the owners of Sandy Lane are called away, everyone still expects the stables to run smoothly in their absence. No one is quite prepared for all the things that happen over the next few weeks. There isn't time to get help, the children of Sandy Lane have to act fast, if they want to save their stables...

The Midnight Horse by Michelle Bates

The fourth title in the Sandy Lane Stables series

The horse cantered gracefully around
the paddock in long easy strides, his tail
held high, the crest of his neck arched.
His jet-black coat contrasted sharply
with the white frost, his hooves hardly
seemed to touch the ground as he danced
forward...

Riding at the Hawthorn Horse Trials is all that Kate
has dreamed of and this year she's in with a real
chance of winning. As she works hard to prepare for
the day, it seems nothing will distract her from her
goal. But then the mysterious midnight horse rides
into Kate's life, and suddenly everything changes...

Dream Pony by Susannah Leigh

The fifth title in the Sandy Lane Stables series

The girl riding the pony was as well turned out as her mount. "What a sad bunch of old nags," she said. "We saw you picking your way across the cliffs like a load of old grannies. Come down to the Rychester Riding Stables and we'll get you something decent to ride, though come to think of it, these beasts rather suit you..."

Jess Adams loves riding at Sandy Lane Stables but more than anything, she longs for a pony of her very own. But when her wish comes true and she has to stable it at Rychester, is it really the answer to her dreams? Or just the start of a terrible nightmare?

USBORNE
2
SANDY
LANE
STABLES